Katie

sprinkled
secrets

This book is a work of fiction. Any references to historical events, real people, or real places are used fictitiously. Other names, characters, places, and events are products of the author's imagination, and any resemblance to actual events or places or persons, living or dead, is entirely coincidental.

SIMON SPOTLIGHT

An imprint of Simon & Schuster Children's Publishing Division
1230 Avenue of the Americas, New York, New York 10020
First Simon Spotlight hardcover edition June 2015
Copyright © 2015 by Simon & Schuster, Inc.
All rights reserved, including the right of reproduction
in whole or in part in any form.
SIMON SPOTLIGHT and colophon are registered
trademarks of Simon & Schuster, Inc.
Text by Tracey West
Chapter header illustrations and design by Laura Roode
For information about special discounts for bulk purchases, please contact
Simon & Schuster Special Sales at 1-866-506-1949
or business@simonandschuster.com.
Manufactured in the United States of America 0515 FFG
2 4 6 8 10 9 7 5 3 1
ISBN 978-1-4814-2919-1 (pbk)
ISBN 978-1-4814-2920-7 (hc)
ISBN 978-1-4814-2921-4 (eBook)
Library of Congress Catalog Card Number 2015937198

CUPCAKE DIARIES

Katie
sprinkled
secrets

by coco simon

Simon Spotlight

New York   London   Toronto   Sydney   New Delhi

CHAPTER 1

Good Secrets, Bad Secrets

Sometimes I can't believe how much I've changed since I've started middle school. On the first day of school, my best friend, Callie Wilson, dumped me because she didn't think I was as popular as her new friends. But now I have three best friends: Mia Vélaz-Cruz, Alexis Becker, and Emma Taylor, and they are really great.

I used to think boys were just, well, boys. But now I have a sort-of boyfriend named George Martinez.

I used to think it would be really bad if my mom ever got a boyfriend. But now she's dating Jeff—who I have to call Mr. Green sometimes, because he's a teacher at my school—and it's not bad at all.

I used to bake in my spare time. But now

I bake almost all the time, because my friends and I have a real business selling cupcakes—the Cupcake Club.

I also used to be really against the idea of joining a competitive sports team at school. I would just get too nervous about the whole thing, and then I would make all these goofy mistakes. But now, well, things are different.

"Katie, I don't get it," Emma said during lunch in the cafeteria one day. "Why did you join the track team? I mean, it's great, but I thought you just liked to run for fun."

"Well, I was really anxious about it," I admitted. "But Jeff—I mean, Mr. Green—is friends with Coach Goodman, the track coach. And the track team is the one team you don't try out for—anyone can join. So even if I don't run in any races, it might be fun to run with a group of people."

"And Coach Goodman is so nice!" Mia added. "I have her for Technology. She makes everything seem so easy."

I nodded. "Yeah, she's supernice. She took me aside in the hall and said she heard I was a good runner. She said I could come to a practice and check it out. She doesn't put a lot of pressure on the team, but everybody tries really hard, anyway,

2

you know? So it seemed good, and I just thought I should go for it."

"That's really great," said Alexis. Her curly red hair bounced on her shoulders as she nodded. "You know, any activities you do will look great on your college application. It's never too early to start." We all rolled our eyes but laughed because Alexis is always thinking about things like that.

"I think you'll be great," Emma added, smiling. "You're an awesome runner!"

"Thanks," I said. "I don't know how I'll do in a real race, though. Coach Goodman says I should do the long-distance races, the 800-meter or the 1,600-meter. And maybe a relay."

"E-mail me your practice and meet schedule when you get it," Alexis said. "It's getting harder and harder to schedule our Cupcake Club meetings these days."

Each of us in the Cupcake Club brings something different to the team. Alexis is a business whiz and keeps us really organized. Mia is a great artist, and she comes up with amazing cupcake decorations. Emma and I are really good at coming up with new recipes and flavors. (I'm not sure about Emma, but I know that I dream about cupcakes sometimes—honestly. Once I dreamed that these mini marshmallows were dancing around a swimming pool filled with caramel, and then they all jumped in. That's how my famous marshmallow-caramel cupcake was born.)

"Are we still meeting Friday night?" Mia asked.

Alexis scrolled down her phone screen. "Yes. Seven o'clock at my house."

"Can we do it at eight?" Emma asked. "I have a modeling job after school, and it might go a little late."

"Anything exciting?" Mia asked, her dark eyes shining. Mia's mom is a fashion stylist, and Mia wants to design clothes someday. Which is fine with me because she wants to go to design school in Manhattan, and I want to go to cooking school in Manhattan. This way we won't have to say good-bye forever after high school—not that we would, anyway, but I'm glad we're planning to stay close.

Emma frowned. "It's a summer preview catalog, so it's lots of shorts and tank tops," she said. "Which means I have to shave my legs."

Emma was wearing a skirt, and I ducked and looked at her legs. "Seriously? Your hair is so blond you can't even see it."

"The camera sees everything," Emma said in a serious tone. "Plus, they told me to." She sighed.

4

"Dylan says once you start shaving your leg hair, it grows in even more," Alexis said. (Dylan is her older sister, who's in high school.) "And I think she's right. I woke up the other morning, and I swear my leg hairs grew an inch."

The conversation was making me kind of uncomfortable. I had never even thought about shaving my legs. Honestly, I never even noticed that everyone else started doing it.

"I hate doing it," said Mia. "Don't you, Katie?"

Mia is my closest friend. If we were alone, maybe I would have told the truth right then. Instead, I lied.

"Yeah, it's the worst," I agreed, even though I had no idea what it was like. Then I quickly changed the subject. "So, yeah, eight o'clock on Friday is fine with me for a meeting."

"Me too," Mia said.

"Then eight o'clock it is," Alexis said, typing into her phone. She put it down and opened up her lunch container. "Mmm, Asian chicken salad. Gotta make a note to thank Dad."

"Yeah, he's getting pretty creative with your lunches," I said.

"Once I pointed out that packing lunch was cheaper than buying lunch in the cafeteria every day, he gave in," she said. "I give him a shopping list to make things easier."

Emma poked at the spaghetti on her plate. "Well, I kind of like the cafeteria food. But now I have nobody to wait with on the lunch line."

"Sorry, Emma. I didn't think of that," Alexis said.

"I'd eat the school lunch, but I think packing lunch for me is one of Mom's hobbies," I said. I opened up my new bento box, which is a kind of Japanese lunch box. There are little compartments and containers, so you can have lots of different tastes in one meal.

"See? Carrot sticks and ranch dip, and she made me homemade cucumber sushi, and a hard-boiled egg, and grapes with a sweet dipping sauce."

"That is impressive," Mia said. "I've got a turkey and Swiss on a spinach wrap. Not superexciting, but it's my favorite, so . . ." She shrugged and took a bite. Then her cell phone made a chirping noise.

Mia picked it up and looked at the screen. Her eyes went wide.

"No way!" she said, shaking her head.

"Who's it from?" I asked.

"Olivia Allen," she replied. "She says that Julie Fletcher was seen at the mall with Todd Weiser."

"So?" I asked.

"So?" Mia said loudly. "Everybody knows that Todd is seeing Bella Kovacs!"

"Why would Olivia be texting that?" asked Emma. "Isn't Bella supposed to be her friend?"

Olivia and Bella are in a club together—the Best Friends Club. Callie (my former best friend) and Maggie Rodriguez are in it too. You have to be really popular to be in the BFC. I think you have to be a little mean, too, but some of them are nicer than others. Mia could be in the club if she wanted to, but she'd rather stick with us. (Which is another reason I love her.)

"Well, Olivia is not exactly what you'd call great friend material," Mia pointed out, and we all nodded. When she first came to Park Street Middle School, Mia had been really nice to her. But Olivia didn't appreciate it one bit, and she ended up doing some really mean things to Mia. So Mia ended their friendship. Olivia has been a little nicer lately. But she'll never be one of the Cupcakers.

"You can say that again," I said. "She's not great at keeping a secret, either."

Mia laughed. "You're right, Katie, but since when are you good at keeping secrets?"

I was shocked. "What do you mean?"

"I know what she means," said Alexis, looking

7

at me. "Like that time Emma, you, and I chipped in to get Mia that cool professional sketching kit for her birthday, and we wanted to keep it a surprise, but you blurted it out a week before the party."

I blushed. That had definitely happened. "Okay, well, that was because I was superexcited and couldn't control myself," I admitted. "But I didn't do it to hurt anybody's feelings. Olivia might have seen Julie and Todd at the mall, but she didn't have to say anything. Or she could have told Bella privately, instead of texting everybody."

Emma nodded. "Katie's right. Sometimes when you tell a secret, it can really hurt somebody."

"But sometimes you have to tell a secret, if it means it will keep somebody from being hurt," Mia pointed out.

"Well, I hate secrets," Alexis announced. "I mean, birthday surprises and stuff are okay, I guess. But I think if everybody were honest with one another all the time, it would save a lot of hurt feelings and trouble, you know?"

"Exactly," I said. "Some secrets are good, and some secrets are bad."

I looked over at the BFC table. Olivia and Bella were sitting next to each other, and Bella was laughing about something. She had no idea that Olivia was spreading rumors that might hurt her.

Mia saw me looking at Bella.

"Yeah, I guess that text was a pretty bad one," she said. "Gossip can be really fun, but I guess it mostly stinks, you know?"

"Definitely," I agreed. "You know, I'm really glad we all don't keep secrets from one another." Then I briefly thought of the lie I had told about shaving my legs just minutes before—but that didn't count, did it? It was just a little white lie.

"Me too," my friends agreed, pretty much at the same time.

We finished our lunch and didn't talk about secrets anymore. That's because none of us knew it yet, but secrets were about to nearly tear apart the Cupcake Club.

silly legs!

CHAPTER 2

Did She Really Say That?

$\mathcal{M}$y first track practice was the next day, right after school. I was worried about things like whether I would be good enough or fast enough for the team. I wasn't thinking about secrets at all that first day—but as it turns out, maybe I should have.

Both the boys' and girls' teams practiced at the middle school field. There's a track that goes around the field for the running events, and the events like the shot put and long jump take place on the field part. Coach Goodman had told me to go to the girls' locker room to change before practice each day.

When I got to the locker room, I scanned to see who else I knew who was on the team. There was Hana Hancock, from my drama class. She was one of the tallest girls in our grade, and I figured that would make her a pretty good runner. I'm not supershort or supertall, just average, but I know I could probably run faster with long legs like Hana's.

Then I saw Natalie Egan, who's in my Spanish class. She's almost as tall as Hana, and I started to get nervous. Was I too short for the track team? Was there even such a thing as being too short for the track team? What if I lost every single race? What if I started too early or tripped? My mind started racing.

You're just being silly, Katie, I told myself. *There are plenty of girls in the locker room who are shorter than you are. Stop worrying!*

While I was having this conversation with myself, I heard a voice behind me.

"Hi, Katie!"

I spun around to see a girl with blue eyes and long blond hair in a ponytail. It was Callie, my former best friend.

"So, I heard you were joining the team," she said. "I guess it's true."

"Yeah, Coach Goodman convinced me," I replied. "She's really nice."

Callie nodded. "Yeah, she is. Well, glad you're

on the team." Then she walked away to talk to some other girls.

That's how things are with Callie and me these days. Friendly, but nothing more. Our days of being besties are over. For a while, I was pretty mad at her, and she was not so nice to me. But we got over that stuff and made a kind of truce. I was actually glad she was on the team too. We're almost exactly the same height, so I didn't feel so short anymore.

I quickly changed into blue shorts, running shoes, and my official blue Park Street Middle School track team T-shirt. It felt pretty good to put it on, but scary at the same time. I took a deep breath and followed the other girls outside.

It was a chilly spring afternoon, and I shivered a little. But I knew that soon enough I would be starting to sweat. Coach Goodman walked up to us, wearing a blue tracksuit. She has red curly hair that reminds me of Alexis's. Today, she kept it pulled back with a light blue bandana.

"Hello, girls' track team!" she said with a friendly smile. "Let's give a big cheer for our first practice of the year!"

We all clapped and yelled, "Wooooo!" Then Coach Goodman clapped her hands together. We settled down and paid attention.

"Okay, so for these first few practices we're going to work on form," she said. "Before we start drills, let's warm up and go for a jog."

She led us to a small grassy area near the main field to start stretches, and then we headed onto the track.

"This is not a race!" Coach Goodman called out as she led us around the track. "We just want to get your heart pumping."

It was one of those days when it just felt good to be outside. There were fluffy white clouds in the sky, and the silver bleachers on the side of the track looked shiny and clean and ready for the season. Somehow, I ended up jogging right between Hana and Natalie. I guess we were all keeping the same pace.

"Hey, Katie!" Natalie said, giving me a friendly smile.

"You know Katie?" asked Hana. "I know her too."

"Awesome," said Natalie.

"So, were you guys both on the team before?" I asked.

Hana nodded. "Since we started middle school."

"Coach Goodman seems nice," I said.

"She is," Natalie agreed. "She makes us work

hard, but she's not mean about it. She's a good coach."

When the jog ended, I was feeling pretty good, and I wasn't out of breath or anything. I run with my mom all the time. We run together a lot of weekends. We'll just throw on our gear and head over to our local park. We've even done races and stuff.

Then Coach Goodman had us line up on the track using the lanes. I stuck with Hana and Natalie and got behind them.

"Form drills might seem weird or boring, but we do them for a reason," said Coach Goodman. "They'll help develop certain muscle groups to give you a better stride, make you a better runner, and prevent you from getting injured."

I started to get a little nervous. I thought running was just . . . running. What was all this about form and muscle groups?

"We'll start out with some high knees," said Coach Goodman. "For now, keep your hands still on your sides. Stand up straight. Now, lift up one knee at a time. Kind of like you're marching in place. Left . . . right . . . left."

We all started doing what Coach Goodman instructed.

"Slow now. That's it. Keep your thighs parallel to the ground. Very good," Coach Goodman said.

I looked down at my legs. Parallel? That meant I should keep my thighs straight, like a table. I adjusted my movements a little.

"Okay, now add arm movements," said Coach Goodman, bending her arms at the elbow and pumping them back and forth.

Once we had done that for a while, she told us to go faster.

"Just pick up the pace," she said. "There we go! Keep those knees high."

We did it faster, and I started giggling. I couldn't help it. We all looked pretty silly!

"Glad you're having fun, Katie," called out Coach Goodman, but she was smiling, not being sarcastic or scolding, thank goodness. I smiled back.

Once we got used to the faster pace, Coach told us to start walking while we did high knees. We high-kneed our way around the track.

"We look like prancing ponies," I said, giggling again. Hana and Natalie started giggling too.

"You'll get used to it," Hana promised.

After we'd completed a lap around the track, we lined up at the starting line. I didn't feel too winded,

15

but I could feel a slight burning in my legs. I guess I was developing those muscle groups Coach was talking about!

I thought high knees was a pretty silly exercise, but then it got even worse.

"Okay," Coach Goodman said. "Time for butt kicks!"

"Is that what I think it is?" I asked.

"Yup," Natalie said with a nod.

For the butt kicks, we had to keep our backs straight, facing forward, and kick back our heels so that they almost touched our butts.

Now I can tell everyone that track practice kicked my butt! I thought, and then I burst out giggling. Coach looked over at me and raised an eyebrow, and I turned my attention back to kicking my butt.

When we finished the butt kicks, things got even weirder! We did this thing called high skips, where we had to basically skip as we ran while swinging arms.

"This is great training that will help you push off at the start of a race," Coach Goodman explained as we collapsed into giggles after having finished a lap of high skips. I mean, we looked pretty ridiculous! But even though it was weird, I was having fun.

We did the drills all over again—high knees, butt

kicks, and high skips. As we were skipping around the field again, the boys started to come onto the field. Their practice started right after ours.

I was high-skipping down the track when George, my sort-of boyfriend, walked up to the fence in his blue track uniform. He's on the boys' team, and that was one more reason I'd joined the girls' team. He'd told me how much fun it was. Plus, he'd pointed out that we could spend time with each other at the meets. It'd made me really happy when he'd told me that.

"Hey, look! It's Silly Legs!" he called out.

I wasn't expecting him to call out like that, and I tripped over my own feet, catching myself before I could fall down. Then I stuck out my tongue at him and kept going.

I wasn't offended by what he'd said. George and I have known each other since elementary school. I'm a terrible volleyball player, and he used to tease me by calling me "Silly Arms" in gym class whenever we played. Once I realized he wasn't trying to be mean, the nickname didn't bother me.

But having him yell out "Silly Legs" like that—especially on my first day of track practice—threw me off a little bit. I kept skipping, but I knew I wasn't doing it perfectly. I also knew George was watching me, and I started to feel kind of self-conscious.

After we were done skipping, we did a short jog to cool down and then some more stretching.

"Great job today, girls!" Coach Goodman said. "We're done for the day. See you at the next practice!"

I was sweaty, and I could feel that my hair was plastered to my face. I have wavy brown hair, and I had pulled it back with a scrunchie, but the scrunchie slipped off and my hair was everywhere. Muscles I didn't even know I had were hurting, but it felt good, in a way.

George ran up to me. "Nice job, Silly Legs."

"Please, I don't need another nickname!" I pleaded, laughing. "Maybe I should stay and watch you guys skip around. I bet I could come up with a nickname for you."

George nodded. "Yeah, everybody looks pretty weird doing the form drills. I should have warned you."

I shrugged. "As long we all look weird, it doesn't matter, right?"

"So, are you really going to watch our practice?" George asked hopefully.

I ran through my homework in my brain. Spanish essay, math worksheet, vocab test . . .

"I'd better get home," I said. "Tons of home-work. But maybe next time."

"All right. See ya," George said, and smiled at me before he jogged away. He has the best smile ever and really nice brown eyes, and . . . I really did want to stay, but homework was calling.

I turned and headed into the locker room, and I ran into Callie on the way in. She motioned for me to step aside with her.

"Katie, I'm still your friend, right?" she asked.

"Well, yeah, sure," I replied a little suspiciously. What did she mean by that? I mean, she wasn't *really* a friend anymore. But I guess she wasn't not a friend, either. . . . I was thinking about this, so I guess I wasn't really prepared for what she said next.

"So, how can you let George see you all sweaty and gross like that?" she asked.

I was kind of shocked. I was sweaty, but I had just been running and exercising. That's what hap-pens when you run and exercise. And she thought I was gross? Really?

I shrugged. "I don't know. It's no big deal," I said, but I suddenly felt self-conscious again.

A dark-haired girl appeared in the locker room doorway. "Callie? You coming?"

"Sure, Zoe," Callie replied. "See you later, Katie. Just think about what I said."

I waited a few seconds and then followed them into the locker room. I went to the sink when there was nobody around and looked at myself in the mirror. My face was red and splotchy. My hair was a mess, just as I had guessed. And I had somehow managed to get dirt on my T-shirt, plus the back of my shirt was sticking to my skin, and it was damp and sweaty.

Maybe I *was* gross.

Then I had another panicked thought. My legs! I looked down at my legs. Were they hairy? Is that what Callie meant? Did George call me Silly Legs because they were covered in hair like a billy goat's?

I saw some fuzzy stuff there, but nothing major. Nothing gross. Why would Callie say that, anyway?

I got dressed, figuring I would shower at home. Mom was there in front of the school to pick me up when I left the locker room.

"So, how was your first practice?" she asked.

"Fun," I replied, because that was true. The practice *was* fun.

The part with Callie . . . well, that was not fun at all!

20

CHAPTER 3

Where's My Backup?

The next morning I saw Mia on the bus ride to school, and she asked me the same thing.

"How was your first practice?"

Part of me wanted to tell her what Callie had said, and part of me was reluctant to do that. I mean, the bus isn't exactly private. George usually sits in the seat right behind us. And thinking about Callie's comment still made me feel hurt and weird.

"Pretty good," I replied. "I'll tell you later."

Mia didn't press me, which is another reason why I love her. So we spent the rest of the ride talking about math class and our teacher, Mr. K., and how he tried to do an impression of a vampire guy from some TV show. It'd been awful, but he hadn't minded when we'd laughed.

"I wonder if that's a math teacher thing?" Mia asked. "Does Mr. Green do ridiculous impressions too?"

I shook my head. "He has a pretty good sense of humor, but he never acts goofy," I replied. "Anyway, your stepdad is more ridiculous than even Mr. K. He tells the worst jokes!"

Mia nodded. "This morning he made eggs for breakfast. And then he goes, 'What do you get when a chicken lays an egg on your roof?'"

I giggled. "I don't know. What?"

"An egg roll!" Mia said with a groan. "That's, like, the worst joke ever. But thankfully that's the worst thing about Eddie. He's a pretty good step-father otherwise."

Mia's parents got divorced a few years ago. That's when Mia moved from Manhattan to Maple Grove. Her mom married Eddie, and Mia got a stepbrother, Dan, in the deal too.

My parents are divorced too, but they split when I was just a baby. Mia sees her dad every other weekend and during the summer and on holidays, but I never see mine. I don't even talk to him. That's mostly because he never wanted to, at least up until a little while ago. He reached out and said he wanted to meet me, but I wasn't ready for that then—and I still don't think I am.

If Mom and Mr. Green keep dating, I might get a stepdad too and a stepsister named Emily, who is two years younger than me and goes to my old elementary school. The thought of Mom and Mr. Green getting married was scary at first, but I figure if it worked out for Mia, it can work out for me, right?

The bus pulled up in front of the school, and I saw Callie walk inside with the girls from the BFC and some of the other girls from the track team.

My conversation with Callie came flooding back to me, and I got a knot in my stomach. Luckily, it was Friday, and we didn't have practice again until Saturday morning. But I knew I was going to have to talk about it with my friends before then.

I got my chance at the Cupcake Club meeting we had scheduled for that night.

"So your meeting starts at eight?" Mom asked. "Then maybe we have time to go out to dinner. I've been wanting to try that new noodle bar, Slurp."

"It's called Slurp? We have to go there just for the name!" I said.

Slurp ending up being just as fun as the name

sounded. It was a small place, with bright blue walls and a U-shaped bar with tall stools. The menu had all kinds of noodle dishes on it. You could get rice noodles, soba noodles, or ramen noodles. Spicy noodles or gingery noodles. Noodles with chicken or pork or tofu or veggies.

"It's a noodle-palooza!" I cheered, slurping my slightly spicy noodles with shrimp and bok choy in a yummy soup.

"Yes, they're noodlicious," Mom said, and I groaned.

"That was painful," I said, "but the noodles are good."

Maybe it's weird, but I like going out and doing stuff with my mom. It's been just the two of us for as long as I can remember, and we've always spent a lot of time together. I like being with her, although she insists that once I'm in high school, I won't want anything to do with her. I can't imagine that, but I guess we'll see.

After dinner, Mom dropped me off at Alexis's house for the meeting. Mia and Alexis were already in the kitchen, setting up for our baking session. The rest of the Becker family is just as organized as Alexis is, and their kitchen never has a crumb on the floor or a drop of spilled milk on the counter (unlike my kitchen at home, which is very cozy, but can be a little messy).

"Hey, Katie," Alexis said, looking up as she put tiny liners into the cups of a mini cupcake pan.

"Hey," I said. "Started already?"

"Well, Emma is running late, and Mom doesn't like us in the kitchen after ten o'clock, so I thought we should get started," Alexis said. "I hope Emma gets here soon, because we have a pretty full agenda. I'm anxious for us to talk about our trend reports."

At our last meeting, Alexis had this idea that we should all research cupcake trends to come up with "new ideas that will excite our customers." I thought it was way more fun than any homework assignment I'd had at school.

"Actually, I read this interesting article—" I began, but Alexis held up her hand.

"Not now, Katie! We should wait until everyone is here," she said.

"Okay, no problem," I said. I knew what she meant, because I was on the same page. I didn't want to tell my story about Callie until everyone was there to weigh in.

While we waited for Emma to arrive from her modeling job, we got to work on our cupcake order. Once a month we do mini cupcakes for this bridal shop in town called The Special Day. The owner was one of our first customers, and it's an easy job. The cupcakes are simple—vanilla cake (usually) with vanilla icing. We can practically make them in our sleep.

We had finished the batter and filled the tins when Emma ran in, breathless.

"Sorry I'm late!" she said. "We must have taken a million photos."

"How did the shoot go?" Mia asked.

"Long and boring, but otherwise good," Emma answered. "And I'm glad my mom was there. They wanted me to wear this really skimpy bathing suit in one shot, and she was like, 'No way!' They were cool about it, though."

I made a face. "How skimpy?"

Emma shook her head. "It was ridiculous. But I got to wear a bunch of cool bathing suits with boy shorts and tankinis."

"Tankini? That sounds like a tropical fruit or something," I said. (I don't know anything about fashion. I'm surprised Mia puts up with me sometimes, when that's all she thinks about.)

"That's a two-piece suit, but the top is a tank top," Emma explained, and I immediately knew what she meant.

"Yeah, those are cool," I said.

"Cupcakes are in the oven," Alexis reported. "And Mia's made the icing. Now would be a good time to—"

I interrupted her. "I really need to ask you guys about something. It's about Callie."

That got everyone's attention quickly. They ew my history with her.

"Callie?" Mia asked. "She's on the track team you, right?"

odded. "Yeah, which is basically okay, except this weird thing the other day." I told them he had pulled me aside and made that rude nent. "Can you believe that? She told me I was and gross! And that I shouldn't be around rge like that!"

Mia scowled. "Seriously? What does she know? You are not gross. And George likes you whether you're sweaty or not."

"That's what I thought," I said, relieved.

"Well, she might have been coming from a good place," Alexis said. "I mean, appearance has been linked to athletic performance. Look at the Williams sisters. They always look amazing on the tennis court."

"Yeah, I get it, but why do I need to look

27

amazing? It's not a party. It's track practice," I argued.

Emma had kind of a weird look on her face. She picked up the icing spreader and started tapping it on the table.

"Katie, you are so not gross," she said. Then her eyes looked away from me. "But maybe Callie has a point about George, you know? I'm just saying mean, you and George are practically dating."

"Not really," I said. "I'm not allowed to ha boyfriend yet."

"Yeah, but you know what I mean," said I "You guys like each other, and you go together. So it's kind of like dating. And people date each other, they look nice for other, you know?"

I wasn't sure how to take this. Then I thou about Mom and Mr. Green. When they started da ing, Mom suddenly started wearing makeup a lo more, and she got a whole new hairstyle. She even put on makeup if she was going out running with Jeff. And Mia's mom had taken my mom shopping for new clothes. So maybe Emma was right.

I looked at Mia. "I really need to get dressed up for track practice? I mean, how do I do that? We all wear the same uniform. And I can't help getting sweaty."

amazing? It's not a party. It's track practice," I argued.

Emma had kind of a weird look on her face. She picked up the icing spreader and started tapping it on the table.

"Katie, you are so not gross," she said. Then her eyes looked away from me. "But maybe Callie has a point about George, you know? I'm just saying, I mean, you and George are practically dating."

"Not really," I said. "I'm not allowed to have a boyfriend yet."

"Yeah, but you know what I mean," said Emma. "You guys like each other, and you go places together. So it's kind of like dating. And when people date each other, they look nice for each other, you know?"

I wasn't sure how to take this. Then I thought about Mom and Mr. Green. When they started dating, Mom suddenly started wearing makeup a lot more, and she got a whole new hairstyle. She even put on makeup if she was going out running with Jeff. And Mia's mom had taken my mom shopping for new clothes. So maybe Emma was right.

I looked at Mia. "I really need to get dressed up for track practice? I mean, how do I do that? We all wear the same uniform. And I can't help getting sweaty."

"Yeah, those are cool," I said.

"Cupcakes are in the oven," Alexis reported. "And Mia's made the icing. Now would be a good time to—"

I interrupted her. "I really need to ask you guys about something. It's about Callie."

That got everyone's attention quickly. They knew my history with her.

"Callie?" Mia asked. "She's on the track team with you, right?"

I nodded. "Yeah, which is basically okay, except she did this weird thing the other day." I told them how she had pulled me aside and made that rude comment. "Can you believe that? She told me I was sweaty and gross! And that I shouldn't be around George like that!"

Mia scowled. "Seriously? What does she know? You are not gross. And George likes you whether you're sweaty or not."

"That's what I thought," I said, relieved.

"Well, she might have been coming from a good place," Alexis said. "I mean, appearance has been linked to athletic performance. Look at the Williams sisters. They always look amazing on the tennis court."

"Yeah, I get it, but why do I need to look

27

Emma opened her backpack. "It gets really sweaty under the camera lights. I have this really good antiperspirant that stops me from sweating and ruining the clothes I have to wear."

Mia nodded. "Yeah, I wear antiperspirant too. I totally destroyed one of my favorite shirts with sweat last summer."

I was starting to feel a little sweaty just thinking about it—like the leg shaving conversation all over again. I've never worn deodorant or anything like that. Did I really have to start? How would I know if I should?

"Okay, well, yeah," I said. "That might work."

"And I bet your hair probably gets crazy when you run," Emma said. "If you want, I could do a French braid for you before practice."

That didn't sound so bad. Sometimes it was annoying when my hair got in my face. "I have practice tomorrow morning," I said.

Emma frowned. "I'm dog walking, early. But maybe the next time you have an after-school practice, okay?"

"Sure," I said, but I couldn't help wondering why Emma was pushing the whole thing so much. I was feeling just as self-conscious as I had when Callie had talked to me!

The timer dinged, and Alexis pulled the cup-cakes out of the oven and set them on the counter-top.

"Let's try to get through our agenda while these cool and we ice them," Alexis said.

We talked about our cupcake jobs coming up, and about decorations we needed to get for a kid's party, and then Mrs. Becker came into the kitchen.

"It's getting late, girls," she said. "Think you can wrap things up?"

Alexis looked down at her tablet's screen. "Well, the cupcakes are done. We can do our trend report at the next meeting. But we were supposed to talk about the new flyer I'm working on."

"We totally trust you with the flyer," Emma said. "So we're good."

"Wonderful," said Alexis's mom. Then she looked at our finished cupcakes, all done and packed in a pretty white box with a clear top. "My, those cupcakes look pretty."

"Thanks, Mrs. Becker," I said, and I felt a tiny bit better. I might not know anything about deodorant or hair or shaving my legs, but at least I know I'm good at making cupcakes!

CHAPTER 4

Sometimes Three *Is* a Crowd

𝓘 had track practice early the next morning—like, eight in the morning. I didn't mind so much because Mom and I usually go running early too.

I showed up at the track all ready to go in my T-shirt and shorts. When I got out of the car, I saw a bunch of girls talking on the field, and I ran toward Hana and Natalie. Callie waved to me as I jogged past, and I waved back, but I didn't stop to talk or anything. I was still feeling pretty hurt by what she had said the other day.

"We're going to practice form again today," Coach Goodman announced after she had gathered us together.

Everybody groaned a little.

"You'll thank me later," Coach promised with

a smile. "Now let's start with some warm-up stretches."

We all spread out, and I stood between Hana and Natalie.

"I can't believe we've got to skip around again today," I said.

"At least the boys won't see us," Hana offered.

"Don't they practice right after us?" I asked.

Hana shook her head. "Not on Saturdays. They practice in the afternoon."

I felt relieved. At least if I got sweaty and "gross" again today, George wouldn't see me.

But even though I wasn't worried about the boys, I had something else on my mind. It was a sunny spring morning, and when we were stretching, I looked down at my legs—and gasped.

In the bright sunlight, I could see that my legs were covered with pale fuzzy fur! I looked like a werewolf! How had I not noticed this before?

I quickly looked around, certain that everybody on the team was staring at my wolf legs. Nobody was, but that didn't make me feel better. I felt like I was wearing a giant pair of furry leg warmers.

In a way, I was glad we did drills all practice, because they took my mind off my hairy legs. But as soon as my mom picked me up and I slid into the front seat, I immediately brought it up.

"Mom, why didn't you tell me that I needed to shave my legs?" I accused her.

Mom looked at me, confused. "Honestly, Katie, I didn't think you needed to yet," she said. "Why, have you noticed some hair?"

I lifted up my left leg to show her. "See?"

Mom got close and then squinted. "Oh, hon, that's just peach fuzz," she said. "You don't need to shave that."

"Peach fuzz? *Peach* fuzz?" I wailed, my voice rising. "This is werewolf fur!"

Mom was making that face she does when she's trying not to laugh.

"Does it really bother you? Because there's no rule that says you have to shave your legs," Mom said. "Some women never shave them."

"It bothers me!" I wailed again. (And I know it mostly bothered me because of what Callie said. But right then, it honestly felt like the thing that bothered me most in the world because I had seen it for myself.)

"All right, Katie. If it's bothering you, I can show you how to do it when we get home."

"Okay. Thanks," I said, and then I looked out the window, suddenly feeling awkward. Did I really want to shave my legs? Because everybody says that once you start doing it, you have to do it all the time. And that sounded totally annoying.

But I figured I might as well do it, especially since everybody else was.

"We'll stop at the pharmacy on the way home, and I'll get you your own razor," Mom said. "They make them with the soap already in it, and I think it's an easy way to get started."

Then I thought of something. "Can you get me some deodorant, too?"

Mom nodded and looked at me sideways. "Sure. That's probably a good idea now that it's getting warmer. I should have thought of that." It's weird because Mom generally knows everything, or at least that's how it seems to me. I wondered why it didn't even occur to her to tell me some of this stuff.

We picked up a razor—the kind with the shaving soap surrounding the blade—refills for when the blade dulls, and some deodorant at the pharmacy near our house. When we got home, we went into the bathroom, and she showed me how to do a small part of my leg very slowly. Mom is totally into safety, so she was all business about paying attention and not doing it quickly so I wouldn't accidentally cut myself. Since I don't do too well with blood, I was a little hesitant as I held the razor, but I went up in a straight line slowly, just like she showed me. I thought maybe it would hurt, but I didn't really feel anything at all.

"Okay, I got it," I said. "I can do it in the shower, right?"

"Exactly," Mom said, and then she hugged me. "My little girl is growing up." She was a little teary.

I groaned. "Get out of here, please!" I begged.

Mom left quickly, and I took my shower. I used the razor thing like Mom showed me, and it seemed to work okay except there was a lot of fuzz in the razor. It kind of grossed me out. I washed my hair and kept checking my legs, seeing how unwolfy they were now. I stepped out of the shower.

As I wrapped a big towel around myself, I looked down at my legs. My left knee was bleeding! It wasn't bleeding when I was in the shower! I sort of panicked. I grabbed a tissue and stuck it to where I was cut. Then I ran downstairs to the kitchen, freaking out.

"Mom! My knee is bleeding! I'm—"

I froze. Mom was sitting at the kitchen table—with Jeff!

"Aaaaahhhhh!" I screamed. There I was, wearing nothing but a big towel and a tissue stuck to my bloody knee. How embarrassing! I turned around and ran upstairs to my room as fast as I could.

A minute later, I heard a knock on my door.

"Can I come in?" Mom asked. "It's just me."

"Okay," I said.

"Katie, I'm so sorry," Mom said. "Jeff stopped by to surprise us and to see if he could take us out to lunch. I should have told you he was here."

I still felt totally mortified and miserable. "Yeah."

Mom looked at my knee. "I see you nicked yourself. That happens sometimes. It's nothing to worry about. The blood looks worse because it mixes with the water. See?"

She gently patted the cut with the tissue, and when she took if off, my knee looked totally fine.

I took a deep breath. "Okay. Thanks."

We both looked at my legs. Besides that one cut and a few little patches I missed, they seemed pretty smooth.

"You did a good job," said Mom. I looked down at them again and admired my legs. They looked shiny and definitely not like a werewolf.

"So, do you want to go out to lunch now?" Mom asked.

I thought about having to face Jeff again and made a face. "I'm not sure."

"You have nothing to be embarrassed about," Mom said. "Remember, Jeff is a dad. You were covered up. And he wants to take us to Sweet Sally's."

I perked up. Sweet Sally's has awesome milk shakes.

"I guess I can go," I said bravely. "Just give me a minute."

Mom smiled. "That's my girl."

I came downstairs a few minutes later with my hair still damp and wearing jeans—not shorts.

"Sorry to surprise you like that, Katie," Jeff said, with a smile that was not awkward at all, and it made me feel okay again.

"No problem," I said.

Then we went to Sweet Sally's, which is this really cute little restaurant that sells sandwiches and ice cream. The walls and seat cushions are pink, so it's like a pink explosion when you go in there. I don't mind the pink so much because the milk shakes are the best *ever*.

"So, how's the track team going?" Jeff asked.

"Pretty good," I replied. "I'm a little worried, though, because we're still doing, like, drills, and our first meet is really soon."

"Katie, did you send me your meet schedule yet?" Mom asked.

I picked up my phone. "Not yet. But I have it."

I clicked on my in-box, found the meet schedule Coach Goodman had sent us, and forwarded it to my mom. She picked up her phone and read it.

"Oh wow, there's a meet the day after my birthday," Mom said. "What a nice way to start my day."

I smiled at her. "Cool! It'll be like a whole birthday weekend."

Mom and I have a tradition on her birthday. Every year, we go to the Golden Wing Chinese restaurant and get the pupu platter for two. (It's this tiered tray with all this awesome food, like mini egg rolls and barbecued ribs, and there's a flame on top where you can heat stuff up.) Then we go to the Twisted Cone for ice-cream sundaes, and they always put a sparkler in her sundae and sing "Happy Birthday to You." Then we go home and watch her favorite movie, *The Wizard of Oz*. (We always scream when we see the winged monkeys. They freak both of us out!) It's one of my favorite days of the year.

Mom stood up. "I'll be right back," she said and then headed to the restroom.

As soon as she walked away, Jeff leaned across

the table. He had a serious look on his face.

"Katie, I need your help," he said.

"Um, sure," I replied.

"It's about your mom's birthday," he said. "I'm planning on throwing her a surprise party."

I was definitely surprised to hear that. "You are?"

Jeff nodded. "I got a room at her favorite restaurant and invited some friends, and they're going to decorate the room with her favorite flowers," he said. "I'm so excited! And I need your help getting her there on her birthday."

"On her birthday?" I asked.

"That night," Jeff said. "So what do you say? Can you help me?"

"Well, um," I said. "It's just that, we do this— Yeah, I guess."

I probably should have told Jeff right then that Mom and I had special plans that night. That we have the same plans every year. I was kind of mad he had made these other plans without even telling me first. But he looked so excited, and he had made all the arrangements already, and it sounded nice. . . . I was mad at him and felt sorry for him and sad for me at the same time.

"Thanks, Katie!" Jeff said, and he looked so happy. Then Mom came back and sat down.

"What were you two talking about?" she asked.

"Nothing," I said, and then I took a long, loud sip of my strawberry milk shake. Jeff winked at me, and I looked away.

Now I was just plain mad at him. My day with Mom on her birthday was now totally ruined!

CHAPTER 5

Did He Mean It?

$\mathcal{K}$atie, you have practice after school today, right?" Emma asked me at lunch the following Thursday.

I nodded. "Yeah."

She reached into her backpack and pulled out a hair elastic. "Sit next to me! I'm going to put your hair in a French braid. That way your hair won't get all messy when you run."

I sighed. "I can't stop you, can I?"

Emma grinned. "No."

"You'll look nice with a French braid," Mia said. "Plus, your hair will be out of your face when you're running."

"That's what my scrunchie's for," I protested, moving to the seat next to Emma.

"Your scrunchie has a bunny rabbit pattern on it," Mia said, like that was a bad thing.

"Hey, I love bunnies!" I said.

"So did I, when I was five," Mia shot back. "Now sit still for Emma."

"I am not your pet!" I said dramatically.

Emma stood behind me and pulled my hair back with her hands. She started brushing it out.

"Ow!" I cried.

Alexis looked up from the book she was reading. "Let me guess. Knots?"

"I can't help it," I said. "I can brush and brush my hair, and then five minutes later it's all in knots."

"I don't mind," Emma said. "I don't have any sisters I can do this with. It's kind of fun."

After Emma got all of the knots out, she started pulling at my hair and separating it into strands.

"Are you done yet?" I asked impatiently.

"Not yet," Emma replied.

Mia started dangling a pencil in front of me face. "I will distract you," she said. "Just look at the pencil. Take deep breaths."

I giggled. "That's silly," I said. But then I actually found myself staring at the pencil moving back and forth, back and forth. . . .

"All done," Emma said.

She sat back down. My whole head felt weirdly tight.

Mia held out a mirror. "Oh, Katie, it's adorable. Look!"

All I could see was a face—my face, with hair pulled back so tightly that it looked like I was practically bald.

"Um, yeah. . . ." I wasn't sure what to say.

"The back is the best part," Emma said. "Too bad you can't see it. But trust me, it came out perfectly."

I wasn't sure how I felt about it exactly, but my friends seemed to like it. So I thanked Emma, and then lunch was over.

My head felt weird for the rest of the day. I'm sure I was probably blowing it up in my mind or whatever, but I couldn't help it. And I was sure everyone was staring at my hair.

After school, I went right to the locker room to change for practice. I walked past Callie on the way in.

She smiled at me. "Your hair looks really nice today, Katie."

"Thanks," I said. "Emma did it."

For some weird reason, it made me mad that

Callie said she liked my hair. Probably because it was just a reminder that she didn't like my hair the way I usually wore it.

Stop thinking about your stupid hair, Katie! I told myself. I was starting to wonder if I was becoming obsessed—obsessed with hair. The hair on my legs. The hair on my head. A week ago, I wasn't thinking about any kind of hair at all. What was happening to me? Aargh!

"Nice hair, Katie."

It was Natalie. And she had such a genuine smile on her face that I couldn't even be annoyed.

"Thanks," I said. "So, do you think we'll be skipping and kicking our own butts again today?"

Natalie laughed. "I hope not."

I changed for practice, making sure to put on the deodorant that Mom had bought for me. I noticed I wasn't the only girl doing that, so I didn't feel so weird.

My legs were smooth. My hair was pulled back so tightly that my eyeballs were an inch closer to my ears. My armpits smelled as fresh as a spring morning.

Okay, practice, I'm ready for you! I thought. Or maybe I should have thought, *I'm ready for you, George!*

When we got outside, I saw that today's practice was going to be different. There was a lot more equipment on the field—the bars for the high jump, and the barriers for the hurdles, and stuff like that. And there were two more coaches.

"This is Mr. Parker, Zoe's dad," said Coach Goodman, pointing to a neat-looking guy with close-cropped brown hair. "This is Mrs. Lopez, Belinda's mom."

Mrs. Lopez had a friendly smile and wore her dark hair in a ponytail. She waved at us.

"And they have volunteered to be my assistant coaches," Coach Goodman went on. "Today, we'll start with some warm-ups and some form, and then we'll let you guys try some different events. Okay?"

"Yeah!" we cheered.

So we warmed up as usual, and we did do some skipping and other stuff, but only for a little bit. Then Coach Goodman started splitting us up.

"Katie, Hana, Zoe! Go see Mrs. Lopez about long distance," she told us.

The three of us jogged over to Mrs. Lopez, who was waiting for us on the bleachers.

"Nice to meet you girls," she said. "I know Hana already."

"I'm Katie," I offered.

"And I'm Zoe," Zoe said.

I glanced over at Zoe. All I really knew about her was that she was friendly with Callie. Which could mean she was nice, or it could mean she was a popular girl with a mean streak. It was hard to tell which one she was just by looking at her. She had pretty, thick, brown hair pulled back with a white headband, and some woven bracelets on her wrist. Her running shoes looked like they were brand new.

"So, Coach Goodman says you three might be good for the long-distance races," Mrs. Lopez went on. "Those are the 800-meters, which is about a half mile, and the 1,600-meters, which is about a mile."

"No sweat," Zoe said confidently. "I run three miles a day already."

"And I do too. Well, not every day, but a few times a week," I piped up.

Mrs. Lopez nodded. "Great. These races are all about endurance plus speed. For now, Coach Goodman wants you to start with a fifteen-minute run around the track. Sound okay?"

We nodded.

"Great," said Mrs. Lopez. "Don't worry about speed right now."

We made our way to the track and began to run. Hana and I started off with a fairly slow run, but Zoe quickly darted past us.

"Think she can keep that up for fifteen minutes?" Hana asked.

"We'll see," I said. I guessed Zoe was pretty competitive.

It felt really good to run, except for the fact that my French braid kept bouncing against the back of my neck. *Thump . . . Thump . . . Thump . . .* It was driving me crazy!

After about five minutes, Zoe started to slow down, and Hana and I caught up to her. Then we all pretty much kept the same pace, running in step. Zoe looked over at me.

"Maybe we'll get to do a practice race," she said.

"Yeah, I hope so," I replied. The thought of running a real race without practicing first made me nervous.

Thump . . . Thump . . . Thump . . .

Finally, we passed Mrs. Lopez, and she called out to us. "One more time around the track, girls!"

We picked up the pace a little, and just before we got back to Mrs. Lopez again, Zoe zipped ahead. Then she raised her arms above her head.

"Woooo!" she cheered.

"Nice form out there," Mrs. Lopez told us. "How are you feeling?"

"I'm feeling like I can't stand this braid anymore," I replied, and then I yanked off the elastic and pulled the braid apart as best as I could. That was about when the boys' team ran out onto the field.

"Hey, look, it's Medusa!" George called out, pointing at me.

Medusa is that woman in Greek mythology who had her hair turned into snakes by the goddess Athena. Leave it to George to think of something clever like that to say about my crazy hair. I noticed Zoe was laughing, so I guess I wasn't the only one who got it.

I pulled at my hair. "Stand back, or they'll bite!"

George ran up to me. "Hey, good to see you," he said, and my heart fluttered a little bit.

"Hi, George," Zoe said. "So you know Katie?"

"Of course I do," George said. "Since kindergarten. Katie and I are like . . . friends."

He didn't say girlfriend, and I guess I understood why. George and I had never said we were boyfriend and girlfriend, and my mom has that whole "no boyfriend" thing. But somehow it still bothered me that he didn't say it.

"Okay. See you," Zoe said, and walked away.

"All right, well, have a good practice," I said to George, and started to leave.

"Hey," he said. "Do you want to, maybe, hang out on Saturday?"

"Well, I have this cupcake thing right around lunch," I said. "Maybe after that?"

"Sure," said George. "I'll text you. Tame your snakes before we go, though, okay?"

"Ha-ha," I said, but I felt myself blush. Was he just teasing, or did he really mean it? Was he embarrassed to be around me and my crazy hair? I couldn't tell.

Track practice was starting to get hard after all—and it had nothing to do with running!

CHAPTER 6

Cake Pops Confusion

$\mathcal{R}$emind me to braid your hair again the next time you have practice," Emma said at lunch the next day.

"No, thanks," I said. "It looked nice and everything, but I didn't like how it felt. It kept bouncing against my neck."

"Well, I could try starting the braid higher up," Emma offered.

I shook my head. "That's all right. I'll stick with my scrunchie."

Emma looked kind of upset that I'd turned her down—a little too upset since we were only talking about a dumb braid. I was going to ask her about it, but Alexis started talking cupcake business.

"Everyone can help bake Friday night for the library event, right?" she asked.

Emma, Mia, and I nodded.

"And my dad is bringing me out on Saturday to do the library thing with Katie, so she doesn't have to do it alone," Mia said.

"Thanks," I said gratefully. I know Mia loves the weekends she spends in Manhattan with her dad, and she was doing me a big favor by spending the day here. Emma and Alexis were both busy on Saturday and couldn't help out.

"He even says he'll pick you up so we can go together," Mia added.

"Then we should bake at my house on Friday," I suggested. "That way we won't have to move the cupcakes around too much."

"Sounds good to me," Alexis said, typing on her tablet. "And, Mia, you've got the decorations handled?"

Mia nodded. "I've got everything we need."

The event at the library was a celebration for the kids in the reading club. We have learned that for events for kids, it's always safest to go with chocolate and vanilla cupcakes. No crazy flavors. But we do go crazy with the decorations.

It was Emma's idea to do fairy-tale–themed cupcakes, and we all loved it. Mia sketched out some ideas, and we picked four: a cupcake with a princess crown, a cupcake with a cute pig face on it, a cupcake that looked like a toadstool, and a cupcake with a bear face on it. Besides food coloring, we would need marshmallows for the pigs; fondant for the crowns; and small, round candies for the bears.

"Then we're on for Friday night," Alexis said. "And sorry about Saturday. I've got that party for my cousin."

"And I've got a modeling job that day," Emma reminded us.

"That's okay," I said. "Mia and I will handle it just fine."

The next morning, Mia and her dad picked me up at ten thirty. I had to rush home from practice to get changed, but it didn't take me too long to get ready.

"Nice to see you, Katie," said Mr. Cruz when I got in the car. Mia's mom is very glamorous-looking, and I guess her dad is the male version of glamorous, whatever that is. He has this perfect black hair, and he was wearing these sunglasses that made him look like a movie star. I used to wonder why he and Mia's mom got divorced, because they're so much alike, but Mia says that was part of the problem. It's too bad. They seemed like a great couple.

"They can both be stubborn, and so they didn't like to compromise," Mia had told me in that way of hers that makes her seem so much more sophisticated than anyone else in Maple Grove. Sometimes I still can't believe we're best friends, but maybe the reason it works is because we are so different.

Anyway, Mia and I looked somewhat alike today, because we both wore our pink Cupcake Club T-shirts, which had the cupcake logo that Mia designed. We had our hair pulled back into ponytails, because there's nothing worse for business than a hair in a cupcake.

When we got to the library, Mr. Cruz helped us carry the cupcake carriers inside. Ms. Reyes, the children's librarian, greeted us by the inner entrance.

"Hello, Cupcake Club!" she said warmly. "I'm so excited to see what you made today."

We followed her into the children's library, a bright sunny room filled with shelves of books. She led us to a table draped with a green tablecloth.

"Is this okay?" she asked.

"Perfect," I said, and we put down the carriers.

"Hi, I'm Alex, Mia's dad," Mr. Cruz said, holding out his hand.

Ms. Reyes's cheeks turned pink. "Nice to meet you. I'm Maricel."

Mia and I looked at each other and tried not to giggle. This happened to her dad a lot. Women got all flustered around him.

"I'll leave you girls to it," Mr. Cruz said. "But I'll be right here. I've got a good book to finish, and what better place to read than a library, right?"

"Right!" Ms. Reyes agreed, laughing and giving him a little wave as he walked away.

"So let's show you what we did," Mia said excitedly, taking the lids off the cupcake carriers.

Ms. Reyes gasped. "Oh, how adorable!"

The cupcakes looked fantastic. The vanilla princess cupcakes had white icing and yellow crowns cut out of fondant, a sort of paste that is made of sugar that you can roll out like dough. Then we decorated the ends of the crowns with glitter gel.

The pig cupcakes were vanilla, too. We did the frosting in pink and made pig faces with decorating gel. A marshmallow cut in half made an excellent snout for each pig.

The toadstool cupcakes were the easiest. We made chocolate cake and then used vanilla frosting that we'd dyed red for the tops. Then we piped dots of white icing to make them look like fairytale mushrooms.

Finally, there were the bears (for the three little bears). We used chocolate cake and frosting, of course. Little round chocolate candies were perfectly cute eyes and ears, and we used decorating gel to give eyes and a mouth to each bear.

"We'll set everything up," Mia told Ms. Reyes in a very professional tone. "And you would like us to hand out the cupcakes, right?"

Ms. Reyes nodded. "That would be so helpful. We don't want things to get messy. The librarians and I will be busy with games and making sure no frosting gets on the books!"

"We've got it," I said, and Ms. Reyes gave us a grateful smile and then rushed off.

As Mia and I were setting up, I got a text on my phone. It was from George: Yogurt Grove at 4? Meet you there.

Yogurt Grove is one of those yogurt places that's everywhere now. They have frozen yogurt and a million toppings you can choose from and add yourself. I texted Mom to see if it was okay, and she said it was fine.

Sure. CU then, I texted back.

☺, George wrote.

I liked the smiley face. And he hadn't said anything about my Medusa hair, which was a relief.

"Who was that?" Mia asked, but before I could answer her, the room suddenly filled with dozens of little kids.

We were busy for a while, handing out a cupcake, a paper plate, and a napkin to every kid who wanted one. The bears and crowns were the most popular, and I made a mental note to mention it at our next meeting—Alexis always loved to keep track of things like that. When things started to slow down, one of the moms came up to the table.

"I'm so impressed with your cupcake club," she said. "I was thinking of hiring you for a party next month, and now I'm sold. Your cupcakes are adorable, but I'm going to order some of your cake pops, too."

"Cake pops?" I asked, and Mia and I shared the same puzzled look. "Um, maybe you're thinking of another cupcake business? We don't do cake pops."

"But I'm sure you're the same Cupcake Club," she said. She rummaged through her purse. "I picked up this flyer yesterday."

She handed us the flyer. It was a Cupcake Club flyer all right—the new one that Alexis was in charge of. It had our logo and website and everything on it, and there, in big letters, was the announcement: NEW! TRY OUR DELICIOUS CAKE POPS!

"Oh, of course," Mia said, forcing a smile. "Yes, we do cake pops. Sorry, we're just a little flustered with all these cupcakes to give out today."

"Well, great," the mom said. "You'll be hearing from me soon."

After she walked away, Mia and I turned to each other.

"What the heck is this?" I asked. Besides being surprised, I was a little angry. "Cake pops? We never even talked about that. What is Alexis thinking?"

"I don't know. But we can find out." Mia typed into her phone. "I'm not going to upset her or Emma, because they're doing stuff. But I'm asking for an emergency meeting at my house, tomorrow night."

I nodded. "Good idea! We need to get to the bottom of this."

The rest of the day went pretty smoothly. The library thing ended at noon, and Mr. Cruz took us out to lunch at Vinnie's Pizza. Then he and Mia dropped me off at home, and at three thirty, Mom drove me to the Yogurt Grove.

George showed up in his track shirt and shorts.

"Hey!" he said. "Man, practice was rough today. I'm starving."

"And sweaty," I teased.

George grinned. "Some yogurt will fix that. Come on."

We went inside and each grabbed a cup. I got a medium-size cup, and George got the biggest one. I knew just what I wanted: chocolate and vanilla twist with breakfast cereal, bananas, and cherries.

George kind of went crazy. He put chocolate, coffee, coconut, and peanut butter yogurt in his cup. Then he put one of *every* topping on his yogurt. Sprinkles. Nuts. Fruit. Cereal. Candy. When he went to pay for it, it was, like, fifteen dollars.

"That is insane," I said, shaking my head.

"Insanely awesome," George said with a grin.

"How can you eat all that?" I asked.

"Easily," he said.

"I bet you can't."

"Wanna bet me?" George asked, wiggling his eyebrows.

"Sure," I said. "If you can't finish it, you have to walk me home."

"And if I do finish it, you have to help me with my social studies," George said.

"Deal," I said. And then I watched as George dug into his yogurt like a hungry dog and ate every last bite.

"Not even a sprinkle," he said, showing me his empty cup. He certainly could pack it away.

"I'm impressed," I said. "So, when do you want me to help you with your homework?"

"How about I walk you home, and then we do it at your house?" he asked.

I grinned. "But then we both win."

"I know," George said, and he smiled at me, and I felt warm inside even though I had just eaten freezing cold yogurt.

We walked to my house, and Mom raised an eyebrow when she saw George, but she didn't say anything embarrassing, thank goodness. We did our social studies homework together, which was nice, because I had to do it, anyway.

When we were finished, George jumped up. "I gotta get home for dinner. Thanks, Katie."

"No problem," I said. "Although I don't know how you can eat dinner after all that yogurt."

"That was, like, an hour ago," George said, rubbing his belly. "I'm ready for more!"

I walked him out, past Mom, who was reading a book in the living room.

"Good-bye, Mrs. Brown," George said. "Thanks for your hospitality."

"You are very welcome, George," Mom said. Then George left, and when I turned back to Mom, her eyes were twinkling. I rolled my eyes at her.

"Mom, he's not my boyfriend. I swear," I said, expecting her to bring up the "no-boyfriend" rule again.

"I know," Mom replied. "But if you did have a boyfriend, George would be a good one, I think."

I went up to my room feeling pretty good. George and I had fun together. Mom liked George.

I really like it when everybody wins!

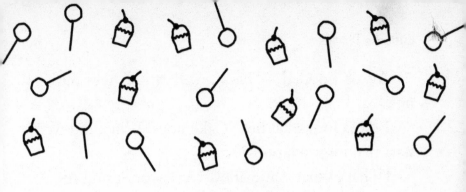

CHAPTER 7

More Secrets?

So what's this emergency meeting about?" Alexis asked the next night as we gathered in Mia's dining room. Mia's little white dogs, Tiki and Milkshake, were running around underneath the table, sniffing our shoes.

"Did everything go okay at the library?" Emma asked.

"It was fine until we saw this," Mia said, holding out the flyer.

"Oh, great, the new flyer!" Alexis said. "I meant to give you some to bring to the library with you. How did you get it?"

"One of the moms gave it to us," Mia replied. "She wants us to do a party and is excited to try out our new cake pops."

Alexis nodded. "That's great! More new business."

Emma looked at her. "Cake pops? When did we start making cake pops?"

"That's what Katie and I were wondering too," Mia said dryly.

At this point, I was feeling a little awkward. Mia seemed to be pretty upset about the cake pops. I hoped this wouldn't turn into an argument or anything.

Alexis seemed surprised by Mia's tone, and she got a little defensive. "Well, I wanted to bring it up at our last meeting, but Emma was late," she said.

"Not that late," Emma muttered.

"And it's a huge trend," Alexis went on. "And we all agreed we needed to try something new. And you guys said you trusted me to do the flyer."

"We did," Mia said. "But adding the cake pops was a big decision. You should have checked with us. We should have put it to a vote."

Alexis held up her hands. "Okay, I get it. But what's the big deal? It's just cake on a stick, right?"

It was time for me to chime in. "Not exactly. My mom and I have tried making them a few times. There's two ways to do it. You can make a cake, and then crumble it up, and mix it with frosting, and then roll it into little balls. Or you can buy a special pan to bake the cake balls in, but that's not exactly the same."

"It doesn't *sound* so hard," Emma said.

"It's not hard," I said. "It just takes a long time. After you make the balls, you put each one on a stick. Then you have to melt chocolate, and then you have to dip each ball in the chocolate, and try to get it even all over. Then you dip the balls in a topping, like sprinkles or something."

"Honestly, I didn't know," Alexis said. "But the flyers are out, and besides that lady at the library, I already got another order for them online. So can't we just try them?"

Mia sighed. "I would rather not. For me, they're not as much fun as cupcakes, because you can't go crazy with the decorating," she said. "And they also take up a lot of time. If you haven't noticed, we're all pretty busy lately. We barely have time to meet and stuff anymore. We shouldn't be making things harder."

"Maybe we should take a vote right now," Emma suggested.

That felt awkward too. We always usually just agreed on everything.

"Or maybe we can just do these two jobs and

then do a vote," I said. "That way we can find out on our own if it's a good idea or not. We'll take down the bit about the cake pops from the website, so we don't get any more orders, and figure out what to say if someone calls to order them if they've picked up the new flyer."

"Good idea, Katie," Alexis said. "Is everyone okay with that?"

Emma and I nodded.

"I guess," Mia said. "I just wish you hadn't kept the cake pops thing a secret, Alexis."

"I did not keep them a secret," Alexis snapped. "I just didn't tell you. And if you want to talk about secrets . . . well, I can spot one of those without needing glasses."

She looked right at Mia when she said it, and Mia blushed. I had no idea what Alexis was talking about or why Mia was blushing. What was going on with those two?

"So, as long as we're together, we might as well talk about those other trends and stuff now, right?" Mia asked, and I could tell she wanted to change the subject.

"Sounds good!" I chimed in, and we had a short Cupcake meeting before we had to go home. I told everyone about the article I read about how nostalgic flavors were coming back, like strawberry shortcake. We agreed we could try some old-fashioned recipes at our next test session.

Thankfully, nothing else awkward happened, and Alexis and Mia didn't seem to be upset or annoyed with each other or anything.

Alexis and Emma left first, and while I waited for my mom to pick me up, I asked Mia, "So, what did Alexis mean about your glasses?"

"Nothing," Mia said quickly, but she wasn't looking me in the eye exactly, so I knew something was up. But I didn't push it.

It looked like the Cupcake Club was baking up a batch of secrets, and that couldn't be a good thing.

CHAPTER 8

On Your Mark, Get Set . . . Go!

On Tuesday, we had our first track meet after school. I had no idea what to expect. Luckily, it was at our own school, so we didn't have to take a bus anywhere or anything. We practiced first, and then a bus pulled up, and the girls' and boys' teams from Greenlake Middle School got out.

"So how does this all work?" I asked Hana and Natalie after we'd finished warming up.

"Basically, they do one event at a time, and they switch between the boys' events and the girls' events," Hana explained.

Natalie nodded. "Yeah, they announce it over the speakers, so you know when yours is coming up, and your friends know when to cheer for you!"

The day before, Coach Goodman had told me she wanted me for the 1,600-meter race, and the 3,200-meter relay. Luckily, Hana was in both events with me.

"We'll stick together, right?" I asked Hana, and she nodded.

"Of course!" she replied.

Natalie made a sad face. "I'll miss you guys. I'll be sprinting. You'll cheer me on, right?"

I struck a cheerleader pose. "N-A-T-A-L-I-E. Go, Natalie!"

She laughed, and I could feel my nervousness slip away just a little bit. Then George jogged up to us.

"Katie, when did you become a cheerleader?" he asked.

"I cheer on demand only," I told him.

"So where's my cheer?" he asked.

I struck another pose. "G-O-E . . . I mean, G-E-O . . ."

George shook his head. "Enough! Stick to track, Katie. And definitely don't join the spelling team."

I blushed. "Hey, there is no spelling team. And, anyway, it's your fault for having such a weirdly spelled name. It's not like it's pronounced 'gee-orge.'"

"Good-bye, K-A-T-I-E," he said, walking away with a wave.

"Good luck in your race!" I called after him.

"Good luck, too, Silly Legs!" he called back.

"He is cute," said Natalie, "but he really likes to tease you, doesn't he?"

I shrugged. "Yeah, it's always been like that. I've known him forever. But he doesn't mean it. It's funny," I replied, but I wasn't sure if I believed myself. Why was he still calling me Silly Legs? In volleyball, I get it—I stink at it. But we weren't doing those silly drills anymore, and I know I'm a good runner. Unless my legs look silly when I run? Or was he talking about how hairy they were? I looked down again—my legs looked pretty smooth, still.

Now I was feeling nervous all over again. Hana sensed it.

"Come on," she said. "They usually do the hurdles first. Let's go watch."

An announcement came over that the events were starting, and as we walked to the first event, I looked up in the stands. Mom had taken off work early to come see me, and Jeff was with her. They both waved and called out my name. I smiled and waved back. It was pretty nice of Jeff to come and watch too, I thought. It was still a little weird at school things like this, since he was a teacher, but no one else seemed to make a big deal about it, so I tried not to either.

The meet turned out to be pretty exciting. I knew somebody in just about every race. I cheered for Natalie during the girls' sprints, and George during the boys' sprints. He came in third!

Then I heard the announcement: "Line up now for the girls' 1,600-meter race."

Hana grabbed my hand. "Come on. It's time!"

We made our way to the starting line. Two other girls from our team, Leah and Kelley, were running the 1,600-meter race too. My palms were sweating, and my stomach was fluttering. This was exactly what I hated about organized sports. For a second, I thought I might turn around and run in the opposite direction.

Then Coach Goodman walked up to us. "No pressure, girls," she said, smiling. "Just tune out everything else and do your best, okay?"

"Okay," I replied, but my voice sounded small.

Silly Legs . . . Silly Legs . . . Silly Legs . . . I couldn't get the phrase out of my mind.

Then we got ready for the race. We had to wear numbers pinned to our shirts. There were eight of us running, and I was number 8. I took my place in the lane with the big 8 painted on it.

Then I waited. The ref calling the race nodded to us.

"On your mark . . ."

Sweat was pouring out of my palms, I swear. I was sure it could be seen from the stands.

"Get set . . ."

I was positive I was going to throw up.

"Go!"

I took off—too fast, at first. I tried to remember what I had learned in practice: Keep a steady pace, and don't burn out too fast.

I took Coach Goodman's advice and tuned out everything. I didn't listen to the people calling out names and cheers. I didn't look to see the runner in the next lane or where Hana was in the race—at least, not until we got close to the finish line.

I snapped back into reality. I could see one, two . . . five girls ahead of me. No way! My heart pounding, I pushed myself to go as fast as I could as I crossed the line.

I put my hands on my knees and leaned over, panting. When I raised my head, Mrs. Lopez was standing in front of me.

"Nice job, Katie," she said. "You came in fourth.

Nice hustle at the end there. Good work!"

"Fourth," I said, panting. I didn't win, but I still felt pretty good. I managed to beat four other people, and it was only my first race.

Hana ran up and high-fived me. "I came in second! That Greenlake runner beat me by two seconds."

There was a break after that, and then it was time for the 3,200-meter relay. I felt pretty loose, and my energy was pumping hard again by then. Coach Goodman had put us in order: Kelley, Hana, me, and then Zoe. I was glad I didn't have to go last!

The relay was a lot less stressful, because although I knew my team was counting on me; it wasn't just me responsible for winning. So once again, I tried to tune out everything, so I could focus.

I was anxious as I waited on the track for Hana to run up and tag me. Each of us had eight hundred meters to run—that's about half a mile; two whole laps around the track.

Hana reached me faster than I thought. I powered off the line, trying to remember the kind of form I was supposed to use. Back straight? Head up? Face forward? Knees high? In the end, I forgot all that and just ran as fast as I possibly could.

I tagged Zoe after two laps, and that was when I realized the Greenlake runner was just a few seconds behind me. She tagged the next runner, who took off like a shot after Zoe.

"Go, Zoe, go!" I screamed at the top of my lungs.

Zoe and the Greenlake girl tore around the track. Everyone on the team was at the finish line now, and we were all screaming our heads off. As the two runners neared, Zoe pushed into the lead. She crossed the finish line first.

"We won!" Hana shrieked, jumping up and down and hugging me.

Now *that* was a great feeling! We had to move away from the track for the boys' race, and then we cheered just as hard for them. They won the relay too!

"Pizza at Vinnie's!" somebody yelled out.

Coach Goodman gave us all a talk, congratulating us and telling us what a good job we did, and Mom and Jeff hugged me and told me what a good race I had run. Then Mom dropped me off at Vinnie's, which was crowded with a bunch of sweaty, middle-grade track superstars.

"Katie, over here!" Hana called out, and I ran to join her in line. I ordered two slices of veggie pizza and a two bottles of water (I was extra hungry and extra thirsty), and then we found seats at the big, long table at the back of the pizza shop.

A minute later, George slid into the seat across from me, carrying three slices of sausage pizza and a bottle of soda. Zoe sat down next to George. Everybody was hyped up from the meet, and they were talking and laughing so loud that I could barely hear my friends next to me.

"Katie, you run pretty good for somebody who eats so many cupcakes!" George shouted across the table.

"They are my secret weapon!" I shouted back.

Zoe leaned across the table. "You're in that Cupcake Club with Mia and Emma and Alexis, right? I went to summer camp with Emma."

"I know Alexis from math class," Natalie piped up next to me.

"Mr. Donnelly's class?" I asked. I knew Alexis was in honors math. "You must be really smart."

Natalie frowned. "This is my first time in honors. It's been really hard, especially with track practice. There aren't enough hours in the day."

I nodded. "Yeah, I can imagine."

"Students! This is a school, not a carnival!" George yelled across the table in a growly voice, and we knew he was doing an impression of Mr. Hammond, the vice principal.

"George, that is perfect!" Zoe shrieked, cracking up.

I launched into my best impression of Ms. Chen, a gym teacher. "Pick up the pace now, people! This is gym time, not nap time!"

Next to me, the sound of a cell phone ring came from Natalie's backpack.

"That's probably my mom," she said, and then she opened her pack and started digging around for her phone. That was when I noticed a paper in there. It had the words "Answer Key" across the top and Mr. Donnelly's name in the upper right-corner.

It got my attention, because Jeff (Mr. Green) is a math teacher, and sometimes he grades papers at our house. I have seen him use an answer key like this before. So for a second I thought that maybe Natalie had one of Mr. Donnelly's answer keys.

But how would she get that? I wondered. And why? To cheat? No way. She's too nice to do something like that. . . . Right?

I couldn't stop thinking about what I saw in Natalie's bag. I thought about it while I celebrated with my teammates, and I thought about it on the bus ride to school the next day.

It was probably just a study guide, I finally reasoned as I got my books out of my locker and walked to homeroom, and I didn't think about it again until lunch. While we were eating, Alexis was studying for her math test in Mr. Donnelly's class.

"Can't you just take a break and eat?" Emma urged her.

Alexis shook her head. "Donnelly's tests are intense. I don't want to blow this one."

"By that you mean getting a B?" Mia teased.

"You say that like it's funny," Alexis replied. "There is no *B* in Alexis. Only *A*."

"And *E* and *I*," I pointed out, but Alexis was back to studying and not in the mood for joking around.

I could see that Alexis was using a study guide, because it said "Study Guide" on top, not "Answer Key."

So is Natalie cheating after all? I asked myself. I thought about saying something, but I stopped. When my mom started dating Jeff, Olivia spread this rumor that I was cheating to get good grades in math, when what really happened was that Jeff helped me study. It felt awful to be accused of cheating when I was innocent. I wasn't about to do that to Natalie. I didn't know her very well, but I considered her a friend. And friends don't do that to one another.

CHAPTER 9

Why Is Emma Acting Weird?

After our emergency Cupcake Club meeting on Sunday night, we didn't have another meeting until the next Saturday. Since we didn't have any orders to fill (except for Mona's mini cupcakes, which are supereasy for us to make), we decided to do a cake pop test. We always test out a new cupcake before we sell it to our customers, so we figured that we should test out the cake pops, too.

We did the test at my house, because we have a lot of baking supplies in our kitchen; if we forget to get something at the store, we usually have something we can use instead.

Mom and I stopped at the store on the way home from track practice to get the extra stuff we would need to make cake pops. I showed everything to Mia, Alexis, and Emma once we were all in my kitchen.

"I didn't get the special cake pop pan, because I think the other way to make them is better," I explained. "First, we make a chocolate cake, and then when it cools, we crumble it up, mix it together with icing, and shape it into little balls."

"That sounds delicious," Emma said.

"It is," I agreed. "I figured we could do chocolate cake and chocolate icing. And then I got some sticks to use and some chocolate pieces that we can melt in the microwave to dip the pops into, so they'll be superchocolaty. And we've got a bunch of toppings we can experiment with."

"So, we start with a sheet cake?" Alexis asked. "Is it the same as our cupcake recipe?"

I nodded. "That should work just fine."

"I'll start the batter," Mia offered.

It didn't take us long to get the cake in the oven. While it baked, we made a batch of chocolate frosting and then washed all the dishes we had dirtied so far. After the cake was done, we had to let it cool.

That was when my phone started going crazy with texts.

From Hana: Everyone from track is going to the mall!

From Natalie: RU going to the mall at 4?

From George: Track team going to the mall at 4. U in?

I looked at the clock. It was one thirty.

"Katie, your phone is on fire," Mia said.

"There's a track thing happening at four at the mall," I said. "I'm thinking I might go. We should be done here in time."

"Is George going?" Emma asked.

I blushed a little. "Yes, George is going."

"Then you should go," Emma urged.

"That's not the only reason I would go," I countered. "Hana and Natalie are going too. Anyway, let me ask my mom."

Mom said it was okay, and by then the cake was cool enough for us to start making our pops. First, we used forks to break up the cake and then put the crumbles in a big bowl. Mia spooned in the frosting, and I passed out thin plastic gloves to everybody, so we could mash up the gooey mix.

"It's like chocolate dough!" Mia remarked.

"It's kind of genius," I admitted. "Cake and frosting mixed together. Yum."

Then we shaped the whole mess into dozens of small balls. I've never golfed before, but I guess you could say they were the size of golf balls. We put the balls on cookie sheets lined with waxed paper, and then we put a stick into each one.

Mia put her hands on her hips and examined them. "They look kind of ugly."

"They're better when they're decorated," I said. "We need to melt some chocolate."

Emma poured the chocolate pieces into a bowl. "Got it."

The chocolate melted in just a few minutes in the microwave, and when we stirred it, the chocolate looked shiny and silky. Then we gathered around and dipped the cake pops in, one by one.

"They're all drippy!" Mia cried.

"You kind of have to twirl them around to get the chocolate on evenly," Alexis offered, demonstrating for us.

"They need to go back on the waxed paper until the chocolate sets," I said. I put the first one down, and then I realized something. "Oh no! We need to get toppings on now, so it can still stick to the chocolate."

I rushed to the counter and started pouring toppings into little bowls—sprinkles, crushed nuts, and these tiny candies shaped like stars. Then I carried them over to the chocolate.

"Okay, here we go!" I announced.

I dipped another cake pop into the chocolate, twirled it around, and then dipped it into the bowl of sprinkles. It was kind of a mess, and the sprinkles only stuck in patches here and there. I had to use my fingers to get the sprinkles to look even. Then I put the finished pop on the cookie sheet, stick side up.

"What if we shake the toppings over the cake pops instead of dipping them in the bowls?" Alexis suggested.

"Good idea! Wait, I'll get plates," I said.

I gave everyone a small plate, so that the toppings wouldn't go everywhere once we sprinkled them on. That worked better, but it was still pretty messy.

Finally, all the cake pops were finished. We let the chocolate set while we cleaned up, and then it was time to taste them.

Mia picked a pop off the cookie sheet and frowned. "Look! The top is all flattened out where the pop touched the cookie sheet."

I picked up another one. That one was flattened too. It was definitely a problem.

"You know, they make these special cake pop holders for display," I said. "Where you put the stick in a little hole. Maybe we could use them for when the chocolate sets, so the bottom doesn't get flat."

"That sounds like kind of a pain," Mia complained, and then she took a bite. "Wow, it's really delicious."

"And you could have so much fun with all the different flavors and toppings," Emma said.

Alexis grinned. "See, I knew these were a good idea. So should we vote?"

I saw Mia's eyes narrow a little bit, so I jumped in before an argument started.

"We still haven't party-tested them," I reminded her. "Let's wait until then."

"That's fair," Alexis agreed.

Then Mom came into the kitchen. "Are you girls almost done? Katie, if you want to get to the mall, we should leave soon."

I looked at the clock. It was already three thirty! The cake pops had taken a lot longer than I had thought.

"It's okay," I said. "We just have a few more dishes to wash, and then I can go."

"Aren't you going to change?" Emma asked.

"Why would I do that?" I asked.

Emma's eyes got wide. "I'm just saying, you're going out, and George will be there, and . . ."

I looked down at myself. My T-shirt had some chocolate smudges on it, and flour dusted my jeans. I guess that wasn't the best look for going out to the mall where lots of kids from school would see me.

"We've got the dishes," Emma assured me. "Now, go change!"

"Okay, I'm going!" I said, although I felt a little insulted. Why was Emma making such a big deal of my clothes? She had never said anything about how I looked before. It was kind of weird.

I ran up to my room and put on clean jeans and a clean purple T-shirt with flowers on it. In the mirror, I could see that my hair was kind of a mess, so I brushed it. Then I ran back down to the kitchen.

"*Much* better!" Emma said a little too loudly.

"Well, I'm glad I pass your inspection," I said with some sarcasm in my voice.

Mom walked in. "If you girls want, I can drive you home on the way to the mall."

"That would be great," Alexis said.

"Hey, do you all want to come?" I asked. I realized I hadn't even thought to ask them, which was kind of rude on my part.

It turns out that everybody had stuff to do, so it was no big deal. After we dropped everyone off, Mom took me to the mall. I promised to not be too late and that I'd text her when I was done. I headed to the food court to catch up with my track friends.

When I got there, Hana waved to me. She was with a bunch of kids, including Natalie, Zoe, and Belinda, as well as George and some other guys from the boys' team.

I joined them, and we all started walking around the mall. Hana and Natalie and I were talking about how hard that morning's practice was when I turned around and saw Zoe and George walking together. Zoe was laughing really hard at everything George was saying.

For the first time ever, I felt . . . I don't know . . . Jealous? Suspicious? It wasn't a good feeling, so I shook it off. George is a lot of fun, and he's nice to everybody in our grade, so why shouldn't he hang with Zoe?

I turned back to Hana and Natalie. A few seconds later, I felt someone run up behind me.

"Hey, Katie!" George said, bumping into me on purpose. "Can you go a little faster, please?"

"Sure!" I said, and then I started running, and George ran after me, and then we just started cracking up, and I felt silly for being worried at all.

CHAPTER 10

More Suspicions

$\mathcal{T}$ ake a look at this!" Alexis said at lunch the following Monday.

She dramatically put a piece of paper down in front of us. It looked like her math test, and there was a big "95" on top.

"You got an A! Great!" I said. "*A* for Alexis!"

"Not that great," Alexis said, sitting down. "I was going for a hundred. I usually get the highest grade in the class, and this time, somebody beat me out."

"Who?" Emma asked.

"Natalie," Alexis replied. "She's the only one in the class who scored a hundred. She got every question right."

She picked up the paper, and for a second I thought she was going to crumple it up and shove it in her backpack. But Alexis is neat, even when she's upset. She slid it into her math folder.

"Oh well," she said. "I can't win them all, I guess."

I got kind of a sick feeling in my stomach, thinking about that answer key I had seen in Natalie's backpack. What if that really was the answer key for the test, and she cheated?

I almost blurted out what I had seen, but I stopped myself again. What if I was wrong? It would be awful. So I decided not to say anything.

That day, Mr. Green was on lunchroom duty. Most of the time, he doesn't come over and talk to me, because I think he figured out that it was a little awkward since kids know he's dating my mom, and he wanted to spare me. (In the beginning, it was one reason why Olivia spread those rumors that I was cheating in math because Mr. Green dates my mom.) But that Monday he walked right over with a big smile on his face.

"Hey, girls," he said. "Katie, I'm excited about the big day on Friday. I hope you're doing a good job of keeping my secret."

"Yeah," I said, poking my fork into the fruit salad in my bento box.

"Thanks!" He held up four fingers. "Four more

days!" He had a big goofy grin on his face.

After he walked off, Mia looked at me. "Katie, you don't seem very excited."

I sighed. "Well, you know how my mom and I do the same thing every year on her birthday, right?"

Mia nodded. "Pupu platter and *The Wizard of Oz*."

"Well, I'm just upset we're not doing it, that's all," I said, suddenly feeling grumpy.

"Why don't you just tell Mr. Green?" Alexis asked.

"Did you see how happy he was?" I protested. "He's like a puppy. And he made all the arrangements and everything without even asking me, so . . ."

"He's nice. He would understand," Emma pointed out.

"Yeah, maybe, but it's too late," I said stubbornly.

"Hey, are we still going after school to get your mom's present?" Mia asked.

"I have practice. Can we go after that?" I asked.

Mia texted someone with her phone. "My mom will take us," she said after a few seconds. "Just tell your mom you're studying or something."

"Okay," I said. *After all, what's one more secret?*

I thought. I couldn't tell Mom about the party. I didn't want to tell Alexis about seeing the answer key in Natalie's backpack. And now I would lie, just so I could get Mom a birthday present. How many secrets was I supposed to keep?

For the rest of the afternoon, I kept thinking about all those different secrets and whether there was such a thing as a good secret or a bad secret. Keeping the surprise party secret: good. Not telling Mr. Green I was upset about it: probably bad. Lying to get Mom a present: not so bad. Not saying anything about Natalie: I'm not sure if that was good or bad, but it felt like a big secret, at least. Not a small one.

So it was a little weird when I saw Natalie in the locker room after school. She was all friendly and stuff, but I wasn't sure how friendly I felt. So I tried something.

"Hey, I heard from Alexis that you did really well on that math test in Donnelly's class," I said.

"What? Oh, yeah," Natalie said, and then she bent down and retied her shoelace. I was pretty sure that she looked flustered. Then she quickly changed the subject. "Are you hungry? I'm starving! All afternoon I couldn't concentrate on anything except my stomach growling." She was babbling a little bit, the way people do when they're nervous.

She probably cheated, a little voice inside my head said, and I pushed it away. And for the whole practice, I did that focusing thing and pretty much kept to myself.

Luckily, going out with Mia that night really changed my mood. I had been so busy with track practice that I hadn't been spending as much time with her as I usually do.

Mia's mom drove us to the bookstore in town.

"Let me guess," Mia said. "You're headed for the cooking section, right?"

"Of course!" I replied.

Mom loves to cook (which is where I got my love for cooking), and I had seen her eyeing this fancy cookbook by this famous chef on her laptop. I had been saving money from my Cupcake jobs so I could get it for her.

There it was, right on display: *Viola's Vegetables*. On the front cover, there was a beautiful photo of a cutting board with fresh vegetables, and inside, on thick glossy paper, were tons of great recipes and a color photo of each dish once it was finished, so you knew what it was supposed to look like. Mia helped me pick out this really nice wrapping paper for it.

"Your mom's going to love it," said Mrs. Valdes. She has dark hair like Mia's, and like I said before, she always looks glamorous, no matter where she is.

"I know she is," I said, feeling proud. It felt great to get it for her with money that I earned myself.

"I am very excited for the surprise party. Mia will be with her dad, but Jeff invited Eddie and me," Mia's mom said as she drove us home. "So I will see you Friday. Boy, Jeff seems very excited about it."

"He sure is," I agreed, but I didn't feel so bad about it anymore. I mean, the important thing was that Mom was happy, right?

Anyway, if I stopped being upset about it, that was one less secret for me to worry about. . . .

CHAPTER 11

Secrets Revealed

There were so many secrets floating around, and I knew they couldn't all be kept secret for long. I was right. The next day, things started exploding . . . and that was only the start of things.

I was eating lunch with Mia, Alexis, and Emma, like we always do, when Bella from the BFC table walked up to our table. She used to be named Brenda, but before middle school started, she changed her name and started dressing like this girl from these vampire movies. She wears dark eyeliner all the time (to look more mysterious or something, I guess), and as she got close, I could see it was smudged, like she was crying.

"Mia! You are such a liar!" she fumed in a voice loud enough for just about everyone in the cafeteria to hear her. She glared straight at Mia.

Mia, as usual, played it cool. "Bella, calm down," she said. "What's up?"

Bella shoved her cell phone in front of Mia's face. "Why did you text Lucy that Todd was seeing Julie Fletcher behind my back? It's not true!"

Mia's face turned pink, and I could tell she felt bad. But she wasn't going to show it if she could help it.

"Honestly, Bella, I don't know why you're mad at me," Mia said. "Olivia texted everyone saying that she saw Todd and Julie together. That's how I found out."

"Olivia is my friend. She would never do that," Bella protested. "Besides, when I asked her about it, she said that you were probably starting the rumor because you were jealous. That you like Todd and just want to break us up."

Mia rolled her eyes. "That is *not* what happened. Olivia is the liar! Can't you see that? I do not like Todd. I like—" She stopped herself. I knew she liked Chris Howard, but she probably didn't want Bella to know that.

"I don't like Todd," she repeated. "He's all yours."

"Then stop lying about him and Julie," Bella shot back.

"Maybe you should ask Todd about that," Mia countered.

Bella gave Mia the most evil look she could manage. "Whatever, Mia. Just stop." Then she turned and stormed back to the BFC table.

Emma, Alexis, and I looked at Mia.

"Wow," Emma said.

"Yeah, that was crazy," Mia said. "Imagine, Olivia blaming me for spreading that rumor. So typical."

"She's the worst," I agreed. "But I feel bad for Bella."

"Maybe if everybody had just ignored Olivia's texts, it wouldn't have been an issue," Alexis said diplomatically.

Mia groaned and put her head in her hands. "Okay, now I feel awful! I should not have been spreading a rumor around. I'm just as bad as Olivia."

"I wouldn't go that far," I said, and Mia gave me a weak smile.

"Thanks, Katie," she said, giving me a hug.

Emma turned to me. "You have a meet over in Franklin, right?"

I nodded. "Yeah. It starts at four."

"Well, Dad's taking Jake to the pediatrician in

Franklin, and he said he'd drop me off at the field so I could see your meet," Emma said.

"That's awesome!" I said. "Thanks. Mom can't get off work, so I won't have a cheering section today."

"I'll do my best," Emma promised.

I was glad Emma was going to be there, because the idea of an away meet made me pretty nervous—we would be in a strange school, on a strange field.

After school, the track team changed in the locker rooms and then got on the bus. Both the boys' and girls' teams fit on one bus. This was a whole new territory to navigate. On the bus ride to school, Mia and I sat in the same row and in the same seats every single time. Now I would have to find new bus buddies.

Just don't say "bus buddies" out loud, I quickly reminded myself. I knew I would never live that down.

"Hey, Silly Legs! Over here!" George yelled from the rear of the bus.

I pushed my way back there. It was a little crazy because everyone was hyped up for the meet. George was in the big backseat with some of the boys, and Zoe was in the seat in front of them. I slid into the seat across the aisle from Zoe.

"Why does he call you Silly Legs?" Zoe called to me.

"Um, long story," I replied. I really didn't want to get into it. Then George jumped into the conversation.

"Because when she plays volleyball, she has silly arms," George said, waving his arms around. "And on the track she has silly legs."

"The first part is true, but not the second," I said. "I only have silly legs during practice. We all do from all the stretching and stuff."

"Ha! Silly Legs! That's pretty funny," Zoe said.

Did I really look silly when I ran? I wondered. I didn't think so, but George was kind of messing with my mind. Luckily, Hana and Natalie came to the back of the bus, and they took two aisle seats. Even though it was still a little weird for me to be around Natalie, I was relieved to see them. I hoped George and Zoe would stop talking about my silly legs, and to my relief, they did.

After about twenty minutes, the bus pulled up to the Franklin Middle School field. I had to admit, it looked pretty much like our home field. The Franklin team was warming up in their yellow uniforms.

When we got off the bus, I immediately started jogging in place to work off some nervous energy. Coach Goodman spotted me.

"Slow down, Katie," she said. "We're going to stretch out first."

Then she raised her voice. "Park Street girls' team! Gather around."

We stretched and then jogged around the track a few times, and then it was time for the meet to start. I looked over to the side fence for the away team and saw Emma there. She waved to me.

"Go, Katie!" she yelled.

I felt a surge of confidence. It really does help when people are rooting for you. I jogged over to see her, because I knew my race wouldn't be up for a while.

"Thanks for coming," I said. "I could use a cheerleader. George kept calling me Silly Legs on the bus ride over."

Emma got a serious look on her face.

"Really? Was he being mean?" she asked.

"Not exactly," I said. "You know how he is. Anyway, I'd better go. My race is soon."

I jogged over to Hana, Leah, and Kelley, and we waited for the 1,600-meter to start. We pinned on our numbers and stretched out, and when it was time for the race, my heart was beating superfast before the countdown.

"Go!"

I tore off, moving pretty fast. Then a really dumb thought hit my brain.

Do my legs look silly?

I looked down at my knees. No, they didn't look silly. But why did I look down? It threw off my pace, and I knew I slowed down a little. I tried to pick up speed again, but I was now in eighth place!

I had to really push myself on the last two laps around the track. Luckily, some of the other girls started slowing down. I passed two girls from Franklin . . . Then Kelley . . . and when I crossed the finish line, I was in fourth place. Again!

"Nice job, Katie!" Hana said.

"I guess four is my lucky number," I said as I tried to catch my breath. "How did you do?"

Hana grinned. "I came in first."

I high-fived her. "Way to go!"

I couldn't help wondering if I might have done better if I hadn't been thinking about my silly legs. I mean, fourth place was decent, but third place would be pretty cool. Or even second . . . or first. Could I ever come in first place on my own and not just in the relay?

Maybe I could, if I kept my head in the game. And that's what I did during the relay—I stayed focused, and this time when I tagged Zoe, I was way ahead of the Franklin runner. Zoe crossed the finish line at least ten seconds ahead of her opponent. She was really fast.

Emma ran up to me at the end of the meet.

"Dad's picking me up in a minute," she said. "Katie, you looked great out there! You guys won the relay! And you finished really strong in that long race you did."

I shook my head. "I think I could have done better. It's George and that whole Silly Legs thing. I let him get inside my head. I've got to ask him to stop doing that. He's got to understand, right?"

"Katie, Zoe likes George!" Emma blurted out, and then she put her hand over her mouth like she wished she hadn't said it.

"What?" I asked. I mean, I was surprised, but not totally shocked. Zoe was always hanging around George. But how did Emma know? So I asked her straight up.

"Zoe told me over the summer, at camp," she admitted. "She knows we're friends, so she asked me to keep it a secret. I didn't think it was a big deal, because George is so into you. But then you joined track, and I knew Zoe was on the team. . . ."

Then it hit me. The French braid. All those remarks about changing my clothes. "Is that why you keep wanting me to look nice? So I don't look worse than Zoe or something?"

Emma looked sheepish. "Yeah, kind of. Since I promised her I wouldn't tell you, I figured maybe I should do something to help give you the upper hand. Especially after what Callie said about you being sweaty and whatever. I didn't want George to start liking Zoe because you were sweaty or your hair was messy."

I was trying to process this. "I get that you were looking out for me. Thanks," I said. "But if George can't deal with me being sweaty, then maybe I don't need to hang out with him."

Emma nodded. "You're right." And then we heard a car horn beep.

"That's my dad! I'll text you later," Emma said, and she waved and ran off.

The team was heading for the bus, anyway, so I jogged to catch up to them. George and Zoe were already on the bus, and Zoe was sitting next to him this time. I sat in the seat in front of them.

George stuck his head over the seat, like he always did on the school bus.

"You came in first on the relay, right? Nice!" he said, and then we fist-bumped.

"How'd you do?" I asked.

"Second in one race, and then I didn't even place in the next one," George said with a shrug. "Next time!"

"Second's really good," I said, and then one of the boys in the backseat grabbed him, and they started wrestling each other. I looked out the window and thought about Zoe.

So, Zoe liked George. What, exactly, was I supposed to do with that information? Wear a French braid and lip gloss to every track meet?

That would be ridiculous, I decided. And just because Zoe liked George didn't mean that George liked her back.

The only thing I decided was that I wouldn't ask George to stop teasing me. I mean, I know he didn't mean anything by it, and I could take it. So why mention it?

Because it bothers you, the voice inside me said, but I pushed it aside. And not telling someone how you really feel isn't exactly like keeping a secret, is it?

Well, maybe not . . . but it kind of feels you are.

CHAPTER 12

A Surprise I Could Do Without

Before I knew it, it was Friday—my mom's birthday. I set my alarm fifteen minutes early so I could wake up before she did for a change. I turned on the coffeepot for her, and then I made a batch of chocolate chip pancakes for us.

The pancakes were turning a golden brown when Mom came into the kitchen in her robe, yawning.

"Happy birthday!" I yelled.

Mom hugged me. "Oh, Katie, this is so sweet. You didn't have to do this. We have our special celebration tonight."

I felt a little pang of guilt. There was going to be a celebration, all right, but it wasn't going to be *our* special celebration.

"Well, I wanted to do something extra special," I said. "Besides, I'm really in the mood for pancakes!"

Mom got a cup of coffee, and I piled some pancakes on plates for each of us. I stuck a birthday candle into her pancakes, and lit the candle, and then I carried it to Mom at the table.

"It's too early in the morning to sing the birthday song," I said, "but you get the idea."

"And now I get an extra wish," Mom said. She closed her eyes and blew out the candle. Then she opened them. "It worked! I have the best daughter in the whole world!"

"Well, I have the best mom in the world," I said, sitting down to eat my pancakes. (Yes, the whole scene was sweeter than the syrup we poured on our pancakes, but trust me, our mornings didn't always go this smoothly. This was a special occasion.)

"So, I made our reservation for six thirty," Mom announced. "Pupu platter for two! I asked Jeff and Emily to join us, but he said they had plans." She sounded a little sad when she said this. I felt a little . . . annoyed again. Mom's birthday celebration was always just the two of us. Why wouldn't she tell me first before she invited Jeff and Emily? I tried to push it out of my mind.

"We'll have a good time anyway," I assured her.

I, of course, knew that Jeff was lying to Mom so he could surprise her. He told me his plan: The restaurant for the party, Mezza Luna, was on the way to the Golden Wing. He was going to call her and say he had left his glasses at Mezza Luna, and then he would ask if she could stop in and get them for him. I was supposed to come in with her, and when we walked in, everyone would yell, "Surprise!"

It seemed like it was an easy enough plan. Jeff came up to me during lunch again, just to go over it. He really wanted everything to be perfect.

"So, remember, Katie," he said. "When your mom goes inside to get the glasses, just tell her you want to come in with her, okay?"

"Got it," I said.

He smiled. "Thanks so much for keeping the secret. You're the best."

As he walked away, Mia said, "You know, my dad gave my mom a surprise party once, back when we lived in the apartment. He had everyone come over while she was at the gym. She was furious! She locked herself in the bedroom and didn't come out until she was showered and dressed up."

"Well, Mom won't be coming from the gym," I said.

"But I'm just thinking, she might be dressed casually if she thinks you're going to the Chinese takeout place. She might feel out of place at Mezza Luna. It's pretty fancy there," Mia pointed out.

"Do you think that would bother her?" I asked.

"It might," Emma chimed in.

I sighed. "Well, it's too late for another plan now. I can't just tell her to get dressed up."

"I know," offered Alexis. "Why don't you get all dressed up, and then your mom will get dressed up to match you."

"If I got dressed up, my mom would think I was delirious from fever and send me to bed," I reminded them.

"That's a good idea, Alexis," Mia said. "Just tell her you're doing it for fun."

"Well, maybe it won't come to that," I said hopefully.

But when I got home from school, Mom was already home from work and dressed in jeans and a *Wizard of Oz* T-shirt. I imagined her wearing that in Mezza Luna, and I knew Mia was right.

"Great shirt!" I said.

Mom grinned. "I knew you'd like it."

"But I was, um, kind of thinking it might be fun to get dressed up tonight," I said.

Mom raised an eyebrow. "Really?"

"Yeah," I said. "I mean, I hardly ever get dressed up, so why not?"

Mom seemed pleased. "That's true. You never want to dress up. Okay, let's do it, then! It'll be fun. I can always change back into my T-shirt later. What are you wearing, Katie?"

I hadn't really thought that out. "My purple dress, I guess," I replied. It has short sleeves and it's pretty plain, but it's comfortable. It was warm enough out that I could just wear it with flats and not worry about stockings.

"Perfect," she said. Then she looked at her watch. "We have plenty of time to change. We need to leave around six, because I have to make a quick stop on the way."

I knew the "quick stop" was actually Mezza Luna and her surprise party. So Jeff's plan was in effect. I went to my room and changed into my purple dress and then brushed my hair and put a headband on. Mom put on a black skirt and a cream-colored blouse and black heels.

She looked really nice, and I was glad my friends had thought of the whole dressing-up thing.

Maybe tonight is not going to be so bad, I thought. At six, Mom and I headed out to Golden Palace, and then she made a turn to stop at Mezza Luna.

"Jeff left his glasses here, and he asked me to pick them up," she said as she parked the car. "I'll just be a minute."

"I'll go with you," I offered.

"That's okay, Katie," Mom said. Uh-oh. I hadn't thought that she'd tell me *not* to go with her.

But I was already out the door. "But it's your birthday. You, um, shouldn't go in alone. And I have to go to the bathroom."

Mom gave me a strange look, but she didn't argue. Inside the restaurant, Mom walked up to the host guy at the front.

"I'm here to pick up some glasses for Jeff Green," she said.

"Right this way, miss," the host said, and he led us through the dining room to a private room at the back. Mom looked puzzled until she stepped through the doorway.

"Surprise!"

I peeked around Mom. The room had a big long table in it, with candles and flowers. There was a pile of presents on a small table in the corner. Everybody was standing up: Jeff and Emily; Mia's mom, Sara, and stepdad, Eddie; the Vallanys, a couple from Jeff's running club; and Mr. K., my math teacher (I guessed that he and Jeff were friends), and his wife. It was a nice-size crowd.

"Oh my gosh!" Mom cried, laughing. "Jeff, you didn't!"

"I did," Jeff said. He pulled out a chair at the head of the table. "Happy birthday, Sharon!"

Mom hugged him and gave him a kiss on the cheek, and then she turned and hugged me. "Katie, did you know about this?"

I nodded.

"No wonder you made me get dressed up!" Mom said. "Now it makes sense."

The last empty seat was between Emily and Mia's mom, so I sat there.

"Hi," I said to Emily.

"Hi, Katie," Emily said. "I am so glad you guys are here! My dad was going crazy."

I smiled. "Yeah, I could tell he was excited about it. He mentioned it every time he saw me."

Emily rolled her eyes. "Yeah, it's all he's been talking about for weeks," she said. "No offense. Your mom's great, but I mean . . ."

"I get it," I said. "Totally."

I guess it was a pretty good party. Mom seemed happy, and all the adults were talking and laughing and getting loud. The food was really good—there was a delicious salad to start with, and then pasta, and then we had chicken piccata, Mom's favorite. (It's chicken breasts in a kind of lemony sauce. Yum!)

The whole time, though, I was feeling a little sad inside. Salad for an appetizer is just not the same as a pupu platter. And Mom was sitting pretty far from me, and it was nice being next to Emily, although she was mostly texting on her phone under the table. I resisted the urge to take out my own phone, but I knew Mom would freak if she caught me. So mostly I was kind of bored.

Then the waiter came in with a big birthday cake with candles on it, and we all sang "Happy Birthday to You" and Mom blew them out. I thought about the sparklers in the ice-cream sundae at the Twisted Cone and felt a little sad again.

"Presents! Presents! Presents!" Eddie started chanting, and everyone clapped. Jeff got up and started bringing presents to my mom to open. I had left mine at home; I wanted it to be the last one she opened, and I couldn't wait to see how excited she would be when she got it.

Mom got a gorgeous scarf from Sara and Eddie, special running socks and headbands from the Vallanys, and a gift card to a coffee shop from

Mr. K. Then Jeff handed Mom a big, rectangle-shaped package. It was wrapped in shiny paper with a big bow.

"It's from Emily," Mom said, reading the card. Then she tore off the wrapping. "How wonderful! It's just what I wanted!"

I couldn't see it at first, and then she held it up: *Viola's Vegetables*. With a big photo of vegetables on a cutting board on the cover.

I felt sick to my stomach. That was supposed to be my gift to Mom. My one surprise for her—ruined! I could feel tears forming in my eyes, so I quickly got up and ran to the restroom.

Normally, Mom would have noticed that something was wrong and she would have followed me. But I knew she wouldn't. It wasn't fair; Emily probably hadn't even picked out that book by herself. I was sure Jeff had bought it and put her name on it. And then there goes Mom, thinking Emily is so wonderful.

I tried to keep it together. I splashed some cold water on my face, and I thought I could keep myself from crying in front of everyone and totally embarrassing myself.

When I got back to the table, everyone was getting up to leave. It took Mom and Jeff forever to say good-bye, and Mom had this dreamy look on her face as we drove home.

"What a lovely party," Mom said. "I had no idea, Katie. Jeff says you knew about the surprise. Thanks for keeping the secret."

"Uh-huh," I said, looking out the window.

"And I can't believe that all of our friends came, and I got such great presents," Mom went on. "How sweet was it for Emily to get me *Viola's Vegetables*?"

I lost it. I just started crying hysterically.

"Katie, what's wrong?" Mom asked.

I didn't answer. I just looked out the window. We were home a few minutes later, and I ran right up to my room and flopped down on my bed and kept crying.

In my head, it was like Mom and I had this special thing, and Jeff and Emily had stolen it away. I know they didn't mean to, but it was still a horrible feeling.

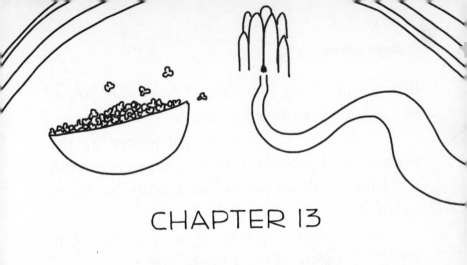

CHAPTER 13

No More Secrets!

Mom knocked on my door.

"Come in," I said through my tears.

I felt Mom's hand on my back. "Katie, is this about our birthday tradition?" she asked.

I slowly sat up, nodding. Mom had figured it out pretty fast.

"Did you tell Jeff?" Mom asked. "I'm sure he would have understood."

"But he already made the plans and invited everybody before he told me," I said. "And he was really excited, and he was doing something nice, and I didn't want to hurt his feelings."

Mom nodded. "That must have been hard for you. But it's important not to hold your feelings inside, Katie. Next time something like this happens, please say something. I don't want you to be sad." She gave me a big hug.

I went over to my desk and picked up the present I had gotten for Mom. This part was still too hard to talk about, so I wordlessly handed it to her.

Mom opened it up, and her eyes got wide. "Oh, Katie!" she said. "What a lovely gift! I know you must have been saving a lot of Cupcake money for this. And how awful you must have felt when Emily got me the same thing." I couldn't speak, so I just nodded.

She hugged me again. "Here's what I'll do. I'll take the copy Emily gave me back to the store and exchange it for another cookbook. But I'll keep the one you gave me. Okay?"

I wiped a tear from under my eye. "Okay."

"And tomorrow, I was thinking," Mom said, "how about we go to Golden Palace? And the Twisted Cone?"

"Fine," I said. "But we are watching *The Wizard of Oz* tonight!" For a second, I thought Mom might say no because it was pretty late, but she didn't.

"I'll go put on my T-shirt," she said.

I changed into my pj's, and Mom and I watched the movie together, and the night ended up not being horrible at all. In fact, when I really thought about it, it had mostly been a pretty nice night.

The next morning, I had a track meet. When I got home, Jeff and Mom were sitting on the front steps.

"Hi, Katie," Jeff said. "I came by to apologize to you."

"Apologize?" I asked. I was kind of mad at Mom. I mean, I should have said something to Jeff, but now that *she* said something to him, it felt weird. I kind of just wanted to forget about it.

"Well, I should have asked if you and your mom had any birthday plans," he said. "In fact, I know she told me about what you guys do every year, but I honestly forgot about it. And then I got all excited with the surprise idea, and I got carried away. I'm sorry if I hurt your feelings."

"Thanks," I said. "They weren't hurt too bad."

"And I was thinking, you and your mom need to keep up your tradition," Jeff said. "She and I can find our own special way to celebrate her birthday on another night. What do you think?"

For a second, I was going to say, "No, don't worry about it," but then I remembered what Mom said about being honest with my feelings and not keeping them inside.

"That would be great," I said, and my mom had a happy, relieved look on her face. Jeff looked pretty happy too, so I figured it was a good solution for everybody.

"Well, I've got to pick up Emily from her music lesson," Jeff said. "Hope you guys have a great day."

Well, we did have a great day! We went to Golden Palace for dinner, and the pupu platter was amazing: three tiers of sizzling Chinese goodness. Then we went to the Twisted Cone and got massive sundaes, and Mom's had sparklers in it, and everybody sang, and it was awesome.

But the day wasn't just great because of all the greasy food and sweet desserts. Mostly it was great because I felt like I had a new philosophy in life: no more secrets! No more holding things in! And I couldn't wait to test it out.

I had my first chance at the Cupcake Club baking session on Sunday. We had to bake for that first cake pop order that Alexis had received after passing out the flyer. The cake pops were due at the party at five, so we started early, at one o'clock at my house. We wanted to make sure that we would have plenty of time to get the cake pops ready. Mia couldn't come at one because she was in Manhattan with her dad that weekend, but by the time she got to my house at around three, we were ready to dip the cake pops in the melted chocolate.

This time, I remembered to get the toppings ready so we could dip the pops in them while the chocolate was still warm. Alexis had also purchased two sets of plastic cake pop holders—one set that we could use to let the chocolate set, that we could get messy with chocolate. The other would be used for party setups, and we would keep those as clean as possible.

"Time to dip!" I said, dunking my cake pop into the chocolate. I picked it up, swirling it around, and the chocolate dripped down my wrist. "This is so messy!"

"Imagine, something too messy for Katie," Mia teased, and I knew she had a point. Normally, messy things don't bother me so much.

We carefully worked to make sure each pop was perfect, gently setting it in the stand to set.

"When these are dry, we can attach a cellophane bag over each one," Alexis said. "And Mrs. Benson wants a purple ribbon around each one."

Now that we weren't busy with the cake pops, and Mia was there, I thought I would bring up my new philosophy.

"So, I've been thinking," I said, "about secrets.

They're no good. Like, I should have told Mr. Green that Mom and I have special plans on her birthday. I shouldn't have kept that inside."

"Right," Mia agreed. "And I should not have shared that text about Todd and Julie."

"So . . . ," I began, "I just want to be honest and say that I don't think doing cake pops is a good idea. They take too much time."

"I see your point," said Alexis. "I should not have put them on the flyer without talking to you guys. But we've spent money on supplies already."

"Maybe we could charge more for them," Emma said thoughtfully. "Then it would make up for all the hard work we put into them."

"I should have thought of that!" said Alexis. "What is wrong with me? I didn't even cost them out. I've been so preoccupied with that math test."

Math test. That reminded me of Natalie—that was another secret I probably shouldn't keep. Before I could mention it, Mia spoke up.

"I like the idea of charging more," Mia said. "We could try it for a while, and if it turns out not to be worth it, we could stop."

"And maybe by then, we'll have made back our costs for supplies," Alexis said. "Sounds like a plan. Does everybody agree?"

We all did. Then I thought of something else. "Alexis, what has been up with you and Mia lately? I swear I've seen you giving each other weird looks."

As if on cue, Mia and Alexis looked at each other, quiet for a minute.

"I'll tell them," Mia said. "It's just . . . Alexis noticed that I haven't been wearing my glasses in class, like I'm supposed to."

"Hey, wait," I said. "I have you in lots of classes, and I never noticed."

"Because you don't notice stuff like that," Mia said. "Alexis does, and she's right—I should be wearing them. But they're such a pain, and I have to take them off to read, and put them back on to look at the board, and then sometimes I just leave them in my backpack."

"Your eyes will only get worse if you don't wear them," Alexis scolded.

"I know. Honestly, I do!" Mia insisted. She turned to me. "So, Alexis feels like she should say something to my mom, and I begged her not to, but then I left my glasses in my locker before seventh period the other day." She sighed.

"I don't want to tell your mom on you, but I'm worried," Alexis said. "I'm your friend."

"So, Mia, just wear your glasses already!" I cried.

She gave me a light punch in the arm. "I know!" Then she turned to Emma. "I know a secret about *you*, Emma Taylor!"

"Me?" Emma looked surprised.

"The other day, I saw you writing this name over and over in your notebook," Mia said. "Nicholas Argenti. You like him! And when you saw me looking, you closed your notebook really fast. Why wouldn't you tell us?"

Emma blushed. "Maybe I like him. I don't know," she said. "But I didn't say anything because Alexis likes him too."

"What?" I shrieked.

"I do not like him!" Alexis cried. "Oh, wait. I think I know what you're thinking. Emma, I told you that Nicholas *Appleby* is cute, not Nicholas Argenti. But I think Matt is cuter." Matt is Emma's brother, and Alexis has had a crush on him forever.

"Nicholas Appleby?" Emma asked, and then she started laughing. "No way. All this time I thought I was betraying you because I had a crush on Nick Argenti. And I felt bad for Matt because . . . well, Matt is my brother."

"So you *do* like him!" Mia accused.

"Yes. No! I don't know!" Emma said and then started cracking up again. When she caught her breath, she looked at me. "Katie, I think you are on to something. It feels good to let secrets out."

"Well, I have one more," I said. "It's something I need to tell Alexis."

"I can take it," Alexis said.

"It's about that math test," I said. "I think I know how Natalie got a hundred on it. I saw an answer key in her backpack."

Alexis nodded. "Yeah, I know. Natalie made a copy of Donnelly's answer key before the test, and she felt so bad about cheating that she confessed to her guidance counselor. The class was getting really hard for her, with track practice and everything, and she panicked before the test."

"No way!" Emma exclaimed.

"Is she in a lot of trouble?" I asked.

"I heard that she might be suspended for a day," Alexis said. "It's too bad. She's really nice. And I get that she caved in under the pressure. That class is rough, even for me."

I let out a breath. "Well, I'm glad she confessed," I said. "That was one secret I really hated to keep."

"So are all your secrets out now, Katie?" Mia asked.

"Almost all of them," I said, thinking of George.

"But I think that's enough for tonight. Unless anyone else has any secrets they want to share."

"No!" Emma, Alexis, and Mia replied at once.

"Then let's wrap these cake pops," I said. "We've got a party to get to."

CHAPTER 14

One Last Secret

Natalie wasn't in school on Monday, so I guessed Alexis was right about her getting suspended. I felt so bad for her!

I was happy to see Natalie on Tuesday, though, because we had another meet, and I knew she would hate to miss it. I saw her in the hall on the way to homeroom, and she looked really uncomfortable, staring at her shoes.

"Hey, Natalie," I said, smiling at her. "Glad you're back." And I meant it. Everybody makes mistakes, and at least Natalie had admitted to hers.

"Thanks," she said, smiling shyly, and I knew that we were going to be cool after that. I knew I could have said something about the suspension, but there wasn't really any reason for me to. Some things you just don't need to say, I guess.

When I got ready for the meet that day, I did things a little differently. I didn't ask Emma to give me a French braid, but the night before, my mom and I went out, and I got one of those special headbands that are just for runners, like the ones she got for her birthday. They come in all different patterns; I picked out a blue one to match my uniform, with peace signs on it. It had a hole in the back of it, so I could push my hair through to make a ponytail, and it kept my hair neat. And it didn't feel weird or anything. I know, because I tested it by running around the store.

I also washed my uniform after practice instead of just stuffing it in my backpack like I do most of the time. And I remembered to bring my deodorant. It wasn't really to look nice for George. And it wasn't because Zoe liked him or because Emma or Callie told me I was a sweaty mess. It was because at Mom's birthday I saw how nice and special she felt when she made herself look good, and I thought maybe that confidence would help me too. If I felt good, it didn't matter what anyone else thought.

I brushed my hair in the locker room mirror and then slipped on the headband. It looked really nice! And it would also keep the sweat off my face.

"You look nice, Katie," said someone from behind me.

It was Callie.

"Thanks," I said. "But, you know, it hurt my feelings that day when you said I looked sweaty and gross. I just want you to know that."

"Okay," Callie said, with a defensive tone on her voice. "I was just trying to be a friend."

"My friends never say I look gross," I said, and then I just walked away. I didn't want to get into any drama before a meet. But it felt good to tell Callie how I felt.

Then I hurried out of the locker room, because I had one big thing to do before the meet started. Luckily, I quickly found George on the field.

"Hey," I said. "Can I talk to you for a minute?"

"Sure," George said. "What's up?"

I took a couple of steps away from the field. I didn't exactly want anybody to overhear our conversation. I took a deep breath.

"I was just wondering," I began. "Um, would you mind not calling me Silly Legs and teasing me and stuff at practice or before a meet? It really throws me off my game."

"Oh man, I'm sorry!" George said.

"Because you don't really mean it, right?" I

123

asked, testing him. I wasn't kidding—I really had to know.

"No! No way!"

"And you don't think I have Medusa hair?" I asked.

"Snakes for hair? Of course not," George replied. "Katie, you know I was just teasing." And he tugged (not too hard) on my hair for emphasis.

One thing was still bugging me. "You don't think I'm gross, do you?"

George stopped dead and stood stock-still and got a goofy look on his face. "Katie, you're the opposite of gross."

Now I was blushing. "Okay. Just wanted to make sure."

Then we heard a coach's whistle, and we ran back to the field to join our teams. I was much calmer than usual at a meet. When I ran the 1,600-meter, I wasn't thinking about anything instead of running, and I came in third place instead of fourth! And our relay team won again.

After the meet was over, a bunch of us were hanging out on the field.

"Hey, who wants to go for pizza?" somebody yelled out.

"That's a good idea," said Zoe, who was next

to George, as she usually was these days. "Are you coming, George? You're always in the mood for pizza, right?"

"I don't know," George said. He walked over to me. "Katie, do you want to get some yogurt with me? I heard they have three new toppings."

"Just me and you?" I asked.

George nodded. "Sure, why not?"

I glanced over at Zoe. She looked a little disappointed, and I knew she had heard George. I felt a little bad for her, but I felt happy just the same.

"Honestly, there isn't anything else I'd rather do right now," I told George. I liked George, and George liked me—and that wasn't a secret anymore!

Want another sweet cupcake?

Here's a sneak peek

of the next book in the

CUPCaKe 🧁 DIARIeS

series:

Mia
the way the
cupcake
crumbles

I Told You I Hate Mondays!

It was one of those dreams that you wished would go on and on. I was at a fashion show, and there were tons of celebrities in the seats. And these models, who all looked like my friend Emma Taylor, were walking down the runway, wearing the most gorgeous clothes. And I had designed them all! Everyone kept clapping and clapping.

Then the dream crowd began to chant. *"Mia! Mia! Mia!"*

"Mia!"

I woke up with a start at the sound of Mom calling my name.

Why is she waking me up? I wondered groggily. She knows I set my alarm every night, and I wake up at six forty-five every morning—in time to get dressed, eat my breakfast, and, most important, do my hair.

I was feeling really cranky that Mom had interrupted my dream—and then I looked at the clock: 7:06.

"Mia, did you forget to set your alarm?" Mom called up to me.

I groaned in reply. Yes, I had, but I hated to admit it out loud.

"Mondays," I mumbled, climbing out of bed. Mondays are bad enough as it is, but they're even worse when you're running twenty minutes late.

I ran into the bathroom and quickly jumped in the shower. Normally, I like to leave my conditioner in my hair for a full three minutes, but I knew I didn't have time. I slopped it on and rinsed it out. It would have to do.

I toweled it dry and quickly got dressed in skinny jeans and a plain black T-shirt—classic, and my go-to look for when I'm in a hurry. And my black flats are the perfect touch.

"Mia! Breakfast!" Mom called again.

"I'll take it on the bus!" I called back down, and then I turned on my blow-dryer so I wouldn't have to hear Mom if she argued with me. I have this attachment that lets me comb and dry my hair at the same time and makes my hair supershiny.

I had just finished the left side of my head when my blow-dryer made this funny wheezing noise. Then it just stopped.

"Come on!" I said, pushing the button in and out. I checked the cord and saw that it was plugged in. Frustrated, I pushed the button again, but it still didn't work.

I hated to admit defeat, but I knew it was broken. Now one side of my hair was perfectly flat, and the other side was starting to dry into a wavy mess.

I ran to the top of the stairs.

"Mom! Can I use your blow-dryer? Mine's broken, and my hair looks weird!" I called down.

Mom came to the bottom of the stairs and looked up at me.

"Mia, your bus will be here any minute. I made you eggs, and you are not going to miss breakfast just so you can make your hair look perfect. Please get down here right now."

"But I can't go out with my hair like this!" I wailed.

"Put it in a ponytail," Mom snapped, and walked away.

I was feeling pretty mad that she wouldn't let me use her blow-dryer, but I knew that the ponytail was a good solution. Or, at least, I thought so, until I tried pulling my hair into the elastic. The wavy side of my head kept puffing out, and it just didn't look right. I tried pulling it back again, and then I put it into a side ponytail, but that looked even worse, so I took it out.

"Mia! Now, please!" Mom sounded exasperated.

I sighed, slipped the elastics into my pocket, and opened my closet. My black flats should have been right there, in my shoe organizer, but they weren't. I checked under my bed and saw a lot of dust bunnies, but no flats.

Then I heard Mom coming up the stairs.

"Okay, okay!" I cried, heading her off before she could complain again. I grabbed the nearest shoes I could find—a pair of brown ankle boots—and ran downstairs.

"Finally," Mom said with a sigh when she saw me. Eddie, my stepdad, was leaning against the counter, drinking his coffee.

"Having a manic Monday, Mia?" he asked.

"Uh-huh," I mumbled. Eddie is really nice, but he is always cheerful, and I just don't have that in me.

You'd think that my stepbrother, Dan, would be the same as Eddie, but he's really not. Dan is into this screaming metal kind of music and wears a lot of very uncheerful T-shirts with flaming skulls on them. He walks to the high school every morning, so he was already out the door when I got down.

I quickly ate my eggs and didn't even have time to brush my teeth before I had to go make the bus. Gross! I slipped on my brown boots, annoyed because they totally ruined the look of the sleek black T-shirt and skinny jeans. Then when I grabbed my backpack and ran for the door, Mom thrust an umbrella into my hand.

"You'll need this," she said.

"Why?" I asked, in a kind of haze, and then she opened the door for me and I saw that it was pouring rain outside. I mean, pouring rain.

"Bus, Mia," Mom said firmly.

Glaring at her, I opened the umbrella and stepped outside. Even the rain felt warm and gross, like dog drool.

I guess it was kind of good I was running late for the bus, because I didn't have to wait long for it to get there. I climbed on and slid down into my regular seat, feeling miserable.

At the next stop, my best friend, Katie Brown, got on and took the seat next to me, like she had ever since our first day at middle school. (That's how we met.) Katie is cheerful and funny, and she usually cheers me up.

But not today.

"Hey, Mia," she said. Then she kind of stared at me. "Cool hairdo. Is that a new thing, half flat and half all wavy like that?"

I was immediately upset. Now, Katie wasn't being mean or sarcastic at all. She doesn't know anything about fashion, really, except what I tell her. She mostly wears regular jeans and T-shirts with flowers or cupcakes on them, and I don't think she even blow-dries her hair. Which is fine, because Katie is adorable and perfect the way she is.

The reason I was upset is because if *Katie* noticed my hair—Katie, who never pays attention to what anybody's wearing or what their hair looks like—then that meant that everyone else at school was definitely going to notice.

"What's wrong?" she asked. I must have been wearing my upsetness on my face.

I sighed and sank down farther into the seat. "Monday," I replied, and that's all Katie needed to hear. She nodded.

"Yeah, Monday," she said. And we didn't say another word until we got to school, because Katie totally gets me. Which is why she's my best friend.

When we got to school, the linoleum floor was slippery and wet from everyone bringing the rain in with them, and the hallway smelled like a big wet sock. I made my way to my locker, self-conscious in my unmatching brown boots and with my bad breath and crazy hair.

Nobody is staring at you. Nobody is staring, I told myself, but of course, I was wrong.

"Nice hair, Mia," a voice behind me hissed. A mean giggle followed.

I didn't have to turn around to know who it was. It was Olivia Allen. We had been friends for a while, but it just didn't work out. Olivia is as much into fashion as I am.

I turned around, anyway, and gave her a quick smile and wave as she passed me in the hallway. That's one rule of mine I always try to follow: If somebody gets to me, I try not to let them see it.

But the morning just kept getting worse. After homeroom, I have math with Mr. Kazinski. He's tall and wears glasses, and he's one of those loud, fun teachers who makes jokes. That definitely helps make math class bearable, but the downside of that is he expects a lot of class participation.

Katie and I sit next to each other in that class, in the middle, which means we're in a prime spot to be called on. Normally, I don't mind, because Mr. K. doesn't make you feel bad if you get a wrong answer, but today I was just not in the mood.

So when class started, I decided to pretend that I was invisible.

He can't see you, I told myself. *You're invisible. As invisible as the wind. As invisible as . . . glass. As invisible as . . .*

"Mia? Earth to Mia?"

The whole class was laughing, and I realized that Mr. K. must have called on me and I hadn't even heard him.

"Oh, yeah," I said.

"Mia, can you tell me how we can find the perimeter of this triangle?" he asked.

I stared at the triangle on the board. I *did* know how to do it, honestly, but everyone was still laughing and I just couldn't concentrate.

"Um . . . uh . . . ," I said.

"Come back to Earth, Mia, and I'll call on you again later," Mr. K. said. "All right, who can tell me how to find the perimeter of this triangle?"

Katie gave me a sympathetic look, and I shook my head. Being embarrassed in class is not a feeling I am used to. And I answered the next question correctly, but still . . .

"Earth to Mia," Ken Watanabe joked as the bell rang and I headed to my next class. How embarrassing!

"Don't feel bad, Mia," Katie said. "Stuff like that happens all the time in Mr. K.'s class."

"I blame Monday!" I said, and then we waved as we headed down two different hallways.

My hall took me to English class with Ms. Harmeyer. I like English class a lot, and we're reading a really compelling book about a girl who lived during World War II. So I was looking forward to second period.

I was, that is, until I sat down, and my friend Nora, who sits next to me, said, "Mia, what's that on your arm?"

I looked at my right arm, which was covered in blue ink. There was a big blob of ink on the desk, but somehow I hadn't seen it when I came in. Somebody's pen must have busted open.

"Oh, great," I moaned. I raised my hand. "Ms. Harmeyer, may I go wash this off?"

She let me go to the girls' room, and I tried to wash it off, but you know how that goes. I couldn't get it off! I scrubbed and scrubbed with a paper towel, but I still had a huge purpley-blue stain on my arm. I must have been in there for a long time because Nora came in and said, "Ms. Harmeyer is wondering where you are."

I turned off the water and sighed. "I just can't get it off."

Now it was Nora's turn to give me a sympathetic look, and I reluctantly followed her back to class.

After English I have gym with Katie, Alexis Becker, and Emma Taylor—my three best friends. Besides being friends, we own a cupcake business together. Cupcakes helped us bond on the first day of middle school, when Katie shared her homemade cupcake with us. Then we turned our love for cupcakes into something really awesome.

It's nice that we all have gym together, because it usually means I end up on a team with at least one of my friends. Today, Ms. Chen, our gym teacher, divided us into four teams to play basketball.

Now, I like basketball, and I'm kind of tall, and I'm pretty good at it. But on that Monday, it was like I had never played basketball before in my life! I couldn't make a single shot. The first time I threw the ball, it rolled around and around the rim like it was going to go in, and then it slipped off to the side! The second time, I hit the backboard in the perfect spot, but the ball nicked the rim on the way in and bounced out. And then the third time, Jacob Lobel slapped the ball away as it soared to the basket—and he's the shortest kid in our class!

Because of me, our team lost: 8–10.

"It's okay," Emma told me, seeing my sad face as we walked back to the locker room. "Everybody has a bad game once in a while."

"It's more than a bad game, it's a bad day," I told her.

Emma frowned. "Poor Mia. But cheer up! Lunch is next. Maybe the second half of your day will be better."

"I sure hope so!" I said.

A Pop What?

Oh, Mia, you still look miserable!" Emma said as she and Alexis sat down at the lunch table with their trays.

Alexis looked at me.

"I noticed that in gym. You just don't seem like yourself. Did you do something different with your hair?" she asked.

"Yeah, it's a new hairstyle called 'My Blow-Dryer-Broke-and-It's-Raining-Out,'" I replied sarcastically.

"Did you try a ponytail?" Emma asked.

"I tried," I said. I took an elastic from my pocket and slipped my hair into a low ponytail. "See how it bulges out?"

Emma got up and stood behind me. "That's

because you're doing a low ponytail. You should try a messy one, like this."

She undid the elastic and pulled my hair loosely on top of my head before slipping the elastic on again.

"Mirror?" I asked, and Emma quickly grabbed one from her backpack and handed it to me.

I looked at my reflection. The messy ponytail looked pretty good. And all my hair was mixed up together, so you couldn't tell which was the flat stuff and which was the wavy stuff.

"Thanks, Emma," I said, feeling a little better. Then I opened up my lunch bag.

"Cupcake meeting today, right?" Katie asked as she munched on a P-B-and-J sandwich.

Alexis nodded. "After school, at Emma's house," she replied. "I have some new business to bring up."

"And I recorded last night's episode of *Extreme Cupcake Challenge*," Emma added. "I thought we could watch it for inspiration."

"Cool!" Katie cried. Of the four of us, she is the most cupcake crazy. "Mom and I went to a movie with Mr. Green last night and I forgot to DVR it."

Mr. Green is a math teacher in our school—and Katie's mom's boyfriend. It's definitely awkward for Katie, but I think she's getting used to it.

"Let's meet in front of the school after the last bell," Alexis suggested.

We all agreed that sounded fine, and before we knew it, lunch was over.

With my new messy ponytail in place, I was feeling a little more confident. And now that lunch was over, everybody had bad breath, not just me (especially anyone who ate the onion meat loaf at lunch).

Maybe Emma is right, I thought hopefully. Maybe the second half of the day will be better!

Katie and I walked into social studies together. I sat in my seat and put on my glasses. I need to wear them to see things that are far away, like when I watch TV, or I'm in class and I need to see the board clearly. I hated the idea of glasses at first, but now I'm used to them. My main pair is very stylish, with thin copper frames. Well, more like half-rimmed frames, with nothing at the tops of the lenses, so it almost looks like I'm not wearing glasses at all.

Our teacher, Mrs. Kratzer, walked in. She's petite and has short hair, and round glasses and she's one of those teachers you'd call "tough but fair"—you know, strict but nice at the same time.

When the bell rang, she gave us a big smile.

"Good afternoon, class!" she said. "Time for a pop quiz!"

Her words hit me like a truck. I couldn't help myself.

"You didn't tell us there was going to be a quiz today!" I blurted out.

Mrs. Kratzer just kept smiling. "That's why it's called a pop quiz, Mia," she said cheerfully. "As long as you've been keeping up with the reading assignments, you should be fine."

She was right—I would have been fine if I had kept up with the reading assignments. The problem was, the latest issue of *Teen Runway* had come out a few days ago and I had been reading that instead of my social studies. (Yes, I know it's only a magazine, but it takes me a long time to get through it. I take notes, mark the important pages with tiny flags, and make sketches when I get inspired.)

I sighed for the one hundredth time that day as Mrs. Kratzer passed out the quizzes. Katie gave me a sympathetic look—her second one for the day—but there was nothing she could do to help me; it was my fault, and I was on my own. I would just have to do my best.

I looked down at the paper and groaned. We were learning about the dynasties from Chinese history, and I had a hard time keeping everything straight in my head. Was paper invented during the Han dynasty or during the Qin dynasty? Honestly, I had no idea.

I made my best guesses—some of the stuff I remembered from class—and handed in my paper. I knew there was no way I would get a good grade on that quiz.

Can this day get any worse? I wondered as I scribbled forlornly in my notebook.

The answer was: Yes! Definitely!

After school, I walked with Emma, Katie, and Alexis to Emma's house. Emma has three brothers—two older and one younger—and usually one of them is around whenever we meet at the Taylor house. Today it was Jake, Emma's little brother. He's a total cutie, with blond hair and blue eyes like Emma.

"Are you making cupcakes today?" he asked, running up to us when we entered the house.

"Not today," Emma said. "We're having a meeting, so we need some peace and quiet."

Jake frowned. "I wanted cupcakes," he said, and then he ran off.

We unloaded our backpacks and gathered around Emma's kitchen table. She put out glasses and a pitcher of water, and Alexis put a spreadsheet with numbers on the table in front of her.

Each of us in the Cupcake Club has a different role. Katie is great at baking and coming up with new flavors. Emma is a great baker too. I'm really good at coming up with cupcake decorations and displays. And Alexis has the most business sense out of all of us. She does the accounting stuff and handles our bookings and schedules. She's super-organized!

"So I have some bad news," Alexis said as we were pouring ourselves glasses of water.

Of course, I thought. *Did I expect good news on a day like today?*

"Our profits were down five percent last month," Alexis went on. "Compared not only to the month before, but to the same time last year."

"Five percent doesn't sound like a lot," Katie said.

"Maybe not, but it's a sign that business might be slowing down," Alexis replied. "Last month, we were down two percent. So we're seeing a steady decline."

"What do we do?" Emma asked.

"Get some new business, right?" Katie asked.

Alexis nodded. "Right. I've got some ideas. We

can do a new round of flyers. It would be great if we could brainstorm some new flavors or seasonal ideas to advertise."

"We should watch *Extreme Cupcake Challenge!*" Emma said. "I bet we'll get some great ideas."

We moved to Emma's living room to watch the show. Jake was playing with some toy trucks on the floor. Emma and Alexis sat on the smaller couch, and Katie and I took seats on the big blue one. I put on my glasses to watch the show while Emma scrolled through the DVR menu on her TV screen.

Then Katie nudged me, holding out her cell phone. "Check out this cupcake site I found. The decorations are amazing."

It's easier for me to see small things without my glasses on, so I took them off and placed them on the couch next to me. Then I took the phone from Katie and checked out the site. It was amazing. I was trying to enlarge a photo of a cupcake with thin, perfectly curled chocolate pieces on top when Jake ran up to the couch.

"Mia, want to see my truck?" he asked, hopping onto the seat next to me.

Crunch!

Jake's eyes got wide at the same time I got a sick feeling in my stomach.

"Uh-oh," Jake said, and he scooted over to reveal my glasses—my very broken glasses. The thin frames had snapped right in half.

Emma swept over and picked up Jake.

"Mia, I'm so sorry!" she said.

"It's my fault," I told her. "I shouldn't have put my glasses down there."

"No, it's my fault for showing you my phone," Katie said. "Then you wouldn't have taken off your glasses."

I would have smiled at Katie if I hadn't felt so miserable. She's so sweet.

"It's okay," I said. "I've got my backup at home."

Actually, I hadn't worn my backup in awhile. When I bought them, I thought it would be fun to have a pair of fuchsia glasses. Yes, fuchsia—that deep, bright pink. I figured they would add a nice pop of color to my outfits. I wore them a few times, but I ended up thinking they made me look silly. My classic glasses blended in with my face. But my fuchsia glasses made a statement—a statement I wasn't sure I wanted to make anymore.

I tried to enjoy watching *Extreme Cupcake Challenge*, but everything was kind of blurry without my glasses, and I had to squint the whole time. Then I texted Eddie to come pick me up and bring me home. When I climbed into the car, all I could think about was going straight up to my room and climbing into bed. I didn't even want to eat dinner.

This was the worst. Day. Ever.

Coco Simon always dreamed of opening a cupcake bakery but was afraid she would eat all of the profits. When she's not daydreaming about cupcakes, Coco edits children's books and has written close to one hundred books for children, tweens, and young adults, which is a lot less than the number of cupcakes she's eaten. Cupcake Diaries is the first time Coco has mixed her love of cupcakes with writing.

Want more

cupcake DIARIES?

Visit **CupcakeDiariesBooks.com**
for the series trailer, excerpts, activities,
and everything you need for throwing
your own cupcake party!

Simon
Spotlight

Still Hungry?
There's always room for another Cupcake!

Katie and the cupcake cure
by coco simon

Mia in the mix
by coco simon

Emma on thin icing
by coco simon

Alexis and the perfect recipe
by coco simon

Katie, batter up!
by coco simon

Mia's baker's dozen
by coco simon

Emma all stirred up!
by coco simon

Alexis cool as a cupcake
by coco simon

Katie and the cupcake war

Mia's boiling point

Emma, smile and say "cupcake!"

Alexis gets frosted
by coco simon

If you liked

CUPCAKE  DIARIES

be sure to check out these

other series from

Simon Spotlight

IT TAKES TWO

If you like reading about the adventures of Katie, Mia, Emma, and Alexis, you'll love Alex and Ava, stars of the It Takes Two series!

A Whole New Ball Game
by Belle Payton

Two Cool For School
by Belle Payton

sew Zoey

Zoey's clothing design blog puts her on the A-list in the fashion world . . . but when it comes to school, will she be teased, or will she be a trendsetter? Find out in the Sew Zoey series: